ADVANCE PRAISE FOR

A TIME TRAVELER'S THEORY OF RELATIVITY

"I needed this book when I was a kid, and a younger me is definitely reading it in some other timeline. Thanks to the Traveler who brought me that copy."

—William Alexander, National Book Award–winning author of *Goblin Secrets*

"This novel will stretch both your brain and your heart at the same time. Find the thread and jump in. You'll be so glad that you did."

—Kathi Appelt, author of more than forty books,including *Angel Thieves* and 2013 National Book Award Finalist *The True Blue Scouts of Sugar Man Swamp*

"This is an incredible book, no matter which universe you're in. I couldn't put it down. One of my favorite debut novels of the year."

—Erin Entrada Kelly, *New York Times* bestselling author and 2018 Newbery Medal winner

"Truly stellar! I cared so deeply for Finn that I too traveled in time and space and arrived back home changed. *A Time Traveler's Theory of Relativity* is everything I want in a book: suspense, surprises, wisdom, and heart. I will be talking about this gem for a long time."

—Jennifer Jacobson, author of *The Dollar Kids*, *Paper Things*, and *Small as an Elephant*

"*A Time Traveler's Theory of Relativity* is a first-rate adventure featuring characters as fully dimensional as the spheres within which they travel and as nuanced as the shifting light through forest trees. Nicole Valentine writes with the deepest understanding not just of science and the possibility of magic, but of the enduring power of love—lessons readers will absorb with ease while rooting for the intrepid Finn."

—Beth Kephart, author of more than twenty books, including *Wild Blues*

"I can't get enough of all the potential ramifications of *A Time Traveler's Theory of Relativity*! Nicole Valentine has taken two knotty subjects and woven them together in an excellent adventure that pulls at the heart as much as the mind. Finn and all his complex family (families?!) have so many stories to tell, and I'm wishing them well on their adventures!"

—Fran Wilde, award-winning author of The Bone Universe series and *Riverland*

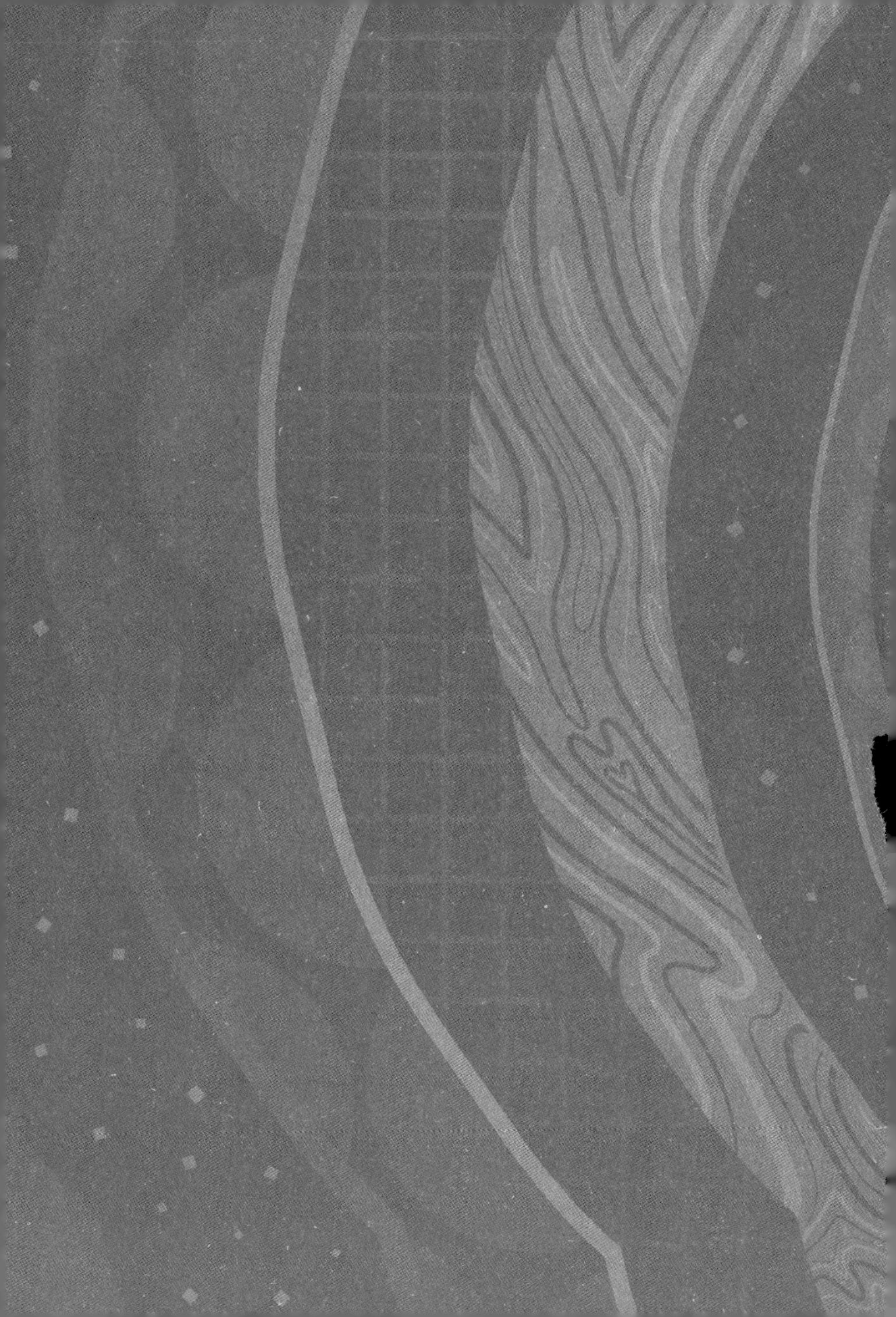

A TIME TRAVELER'S THEORY OF RELATIVITY

NICOLE VALENTINE

Carolrhoda Books®
An Imprint of Lerner Publishing Group, Inc.
241 First Avenue North
Minneapolis, MN 55401 USA

For reading levels and more information, look up this title at www.lernerbooks.com.

Cover Font Credit: Julia Henze/Shutterstock.com.

Designed by Lindsey Owens.
Main body text set in Bembo Std regular 12.5/17.
Typeface provided by Monotype Typography.
The illustrations in this book were created Photoshop CC.

Library of Congress Cataloging-in-Publication Data

Names: Valentine, Nicole, author.
Title: A time traveler's theory of relativity / by Nicole Valentine.
Description: Minneapolis, MN : Carolrhoda Books, [2019] | Days before his thirteenth birthday, science-lover Finn learns that the women of his family are time travelers and he is expected to help locate his missing mother.
Identifiers: LCCN 2018042054 (print) | LCCN 2018049430 (ebook) | ISBN 9781541561076 (eb pdf) | ISBN 9781541555389 (lb : alk. paper)
Subjects: | CYAC: Time travel—Fiction. | Supernatural—Fiction. | Secrets—Fiction. | Missing persons—Fiction. | Family life—Vermont—Fiction. | Vermont—Fiction. | Science fiction.
Classification: LCC PZ7.1.V337 (ebook) | LCC PZ7.1.V337 Tim 2019 (print) | DDC [Fic]—dc23

LC record available at https://lccn.loc.gov/2018042054

Manufactured in the United States of America
1-45998-42839-2/26/2019

FOR LEX, WHO MAKES ME REMEMBER
THE PAST WITH NEW EYES.

FOR DAVID, WHO ALWAYS SEES THE PAST,
PRESENT, AND FUTURE WITH ME.

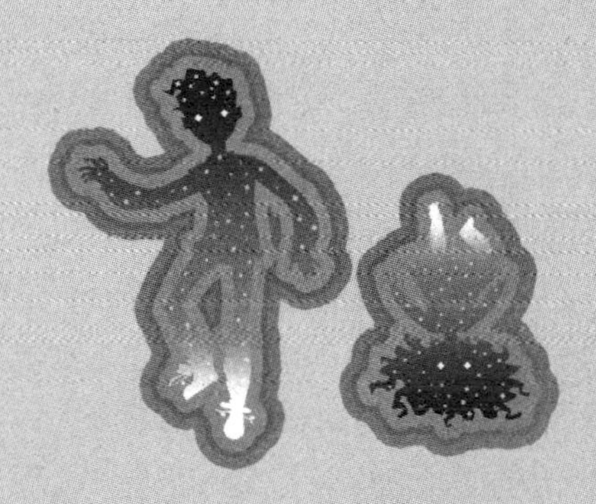

We lie to ourselves when necessary. Some of us are more convincing than others. My family has always been particularly good at it. You see, we deliver our lies in person. One moment you're minding your own business and the next you're staring into your own earnest eyes, persuading yourself to do this or that. It's hard to remain objective when you are face to face with your own reflection. And if you can't trust the one person who should have your own best interests at heart, who can you trust?

There I go jumping ahead again, or was it backwards? No, it was most certainly ahead.

The end is always the best place to start.

I am dying. This old body is finally breaking down. Oh, don't waste your precious time being sad on my account. I've been given more than my fair share of days in this world. And I trust this old crone I've become. I may not like her, but I trust her. All my mistakes are laid out in front of me, plainly seen. Old age has given me that bitter gift, among several others.

I've made things right when I could, even moved a mountain or two when necessary.

But this story isn't about me, not really. It's about Finn. If I succeed, he will have his own future, his own story to tell.

Hopefully he will make things right where I couldn't, because if he doesn't—well, that changes everything . . .

and nothing.

CHAPTER 1

Finnegan Firth slid out of his bedroom window and padded on bare feet across the cold slate patio. He needed to check the mailbox quickly, before Dad's morning alarm went off. Dorset's Lower Hollow Road was the first stop on Mr. Booth's mail delivery route, so the earlier the better. He approached the end of the long, curved driveway and stared down his tin nemesis.

Finn pulled the small door from its latch and was met with a familiar screech of metal separating from metal. Nothing. The box was the same black hole it had been for the past three weeks.

He was not surprised. This disheartening routine had become his new normal.

He stood there on the desolate road, listening to the whisper of the first leaves falling, and wondering if he'd be doing this forever. He couldn't stop himself from hoping, even when all the available data proved he should.

If someone had told him that Mom would leave right before his thirteenth birthday, he would've said it was highly improbable. She and Dad had been arguing more than usual, but there'd been no hint that things were *that* bad. She'd left without leaving a note. She hadn't texted, called, or even emailed since. Finn had tried calling her cell more than once and it always went straight to voicemail. He didn't have the heart to leave any messages lately.

Dad was sticking to the same refrain: she would be back, she just needed time. But as the weeks dragged on, Dad had become more distant than ever. Professor Firth was not an easy man to read, but Finn thought he detected a note of despair creeping into his father's measured responses.

Dad hadn't even mentioned his birthday to him yet. *Watch him forget,* Finn thought darkly.

It wasn't like his birthday was ever a true celebration. In fact he secretly dreaded the whole month of October. It made everyone silent and heavy with gravity. A cloud of smoke-colored grief hung over every birthday cake he could remember. This year he'd be thirteen—while Faith remained three forever.

Thirteen should feel momentous; it should feel like the beginning of a whole new universe. It should start with a big bang. Instead, thirteen was going to be the saddest year yet. Finn was the lopsided remainder in an unbalanced equation, the unstable particle. Always the boy left behind.

He trudged back up the driveway and behind the house. Even the moon wasn't there for him. He was too late. It was already hidden behind the mountain. A few early morning stars remained, twinkling in commiseration. He climbed through his window, pulling the sash down quietly till the rubber insulation met and sealed him inside.

ooo

"Finn, you'd better be packing!" Dad yelled from the living room.

"I AM!"

Finn stood in front of the bookshelf, scanning the spines and doing the math. He figured a three-day weekend at Gran's house meant he'd need four books minimum. It wasn't easy to choose which ones to reread. He had gotten pretty close to recreating all of

Feynman's original Caltech diagrams, but that project was beginning to lose its appeal.

Dad staggered past the open door carrying a large suitcase. "Finn! No daydreaming. You always do this—" He stopped himself. Lately, everything Dad said to him was cut off mid-sentence. "I'm late enough as it is."

Finn bristled. Anyone could see this wasn't daydreaming. It was deliberating. He and Dad had never lived on the same wavelength, but the disconnect between them had gotten worse since Mom left. Mom understood him. She liked to hear about what he discovered in his science journals. At least, that's what he'd always believed.

What if his birthday came and went and he still heard nothing from Mom? Maybe being around him had finally become too hard for her. Maybe *he* was why she left. After all, his very existence was a constant reminder of what she'd lost.

He packed five books to be on the safe side. Carl Sagan was already in his backpack, along with his tablet, which held at least ten articles he'd downloaded from various scientific journals. He'd bring the diagram notebook, too, just in case.

○○○

Dad's car rushed through Dorset's narrow backroads. The patches of dry leaves burst into autumn confetti outside Finn's window. He leaned his forehead against the glass and let out a deep sigh, fogging it up and muting the riot of color outside.

"It's not fair." Even Finn winced at the sound of his voice—like a little kid's whine. But really, why did a man "taking a leave of absence to spend quality time with his son" still have so much work?

"Come on," said Dad, "it's only till Monday. And you love Gran."

"Of course I love Gran."

"Would you prefer I drop you off with one of your great-aunts instead? They're only another five minutes down the road."

He was joking. No parent—even highly disconnected, oblivious Dad—would subject a kid to either one of Gran's sisters. Aunt Ev would vacillate between forgetting Finn was alive and talking his ears off, while Aunt Billie was a nightmare of angles: all elbows, knuckles, and knees topped off with a sharp tongue. Finn had never once seen that woman smile. If it weren't for the nasty comments that sometimes escaped her pursed lips, he would swear they were sewn together.

"I just want to be home, in my own room. Why can't I stay home? I'm old enough."

"No you're not. Twelve is—"

"I'll be thirteen next week."

"I know that, Finn. You think I don't know your birthday?"

Finn didn't bother to answer. He watched the wind whip up a miniature cyclone of leaves. Mom used to call them whirligigs.

"If it gets dull you can call Gabi to come over and visit. Gran would love that."

Right. Sure. Like Gabi wouldn't already have plans with all her new friends. No point in telling Dad that he'd actually messaged Gabi last night to ask if she could hang out this weekend. Usually they'd spend hours texting or chatting online—Finn summarizing articles he'd read, Gabi launching into detailed fantasy book reviews. Lately, though, the exchanges had mostly consisted of Gabi asking if he'd heard from his mom or gotten any more information out of his dad. It was getting on Finn's nerves. Gabi was under the mistaken impression that all you needed to do was ask a question. Maybe that was how it was with New York families like the Rands, but it sure didn't work that way in his.

Last night Gabi had responded to his message with a confusing non sequitur. He had spent a minute trying to decipher her meaning until she typed, "OOPS! wrong window ☺" She never came back.

Finn looked at Dad, who had both hands on the wheel and both eyes on the road ahead. "I want to stay home."

"No deal. You're still too young and Gran is getting old. This way, I know you're taking care of each other."

"Well, that's convenient for you. Split two atoms with one neutron."

Dad ignored his sarcasm. "Did you pack the groceries she asked you to get?"

Finn pulled Gran's shopping list out of his pocket. There were only three small things on the list. He flipped over the paper to make sure he hadn't missed anything. Last time he forgot her Sunday pound cake, and she made him pay for it with a humiliating game of Scrabble. Gran had memorized every high-scoring two-letter word in the English language. She knew a few four-letter ones pretty well, too. Finn learned a lot of vocabulary from Gran. He smiled to himself. The weekend wouldn't be all bad.

"Yeah. It's all in my backpack."

"You somehow found room next to Feynman's entire life's work?"

He didn't want any part of Dad's mocking today—wasn't going to play the *history is more important than science* game. Dad studied what had already happened; Finn studied what was *possible.*

"Can't this trip wait?"

"No, you know it can't." He didn't look at Finn, kept his eyes on the road. "I need to get this paper done and the research reserve is available now at Widener."

"You teach *history.* I'm pretty sure all the facts will be the same next month."

Dad didn't have an answer for that. Finn's mouth screwed up into a painful twist as he bit the inside of his cheek. He kept staring out the window, focusing first on his reflection in the side mirror and then the road behind him. *Objects in mirror are closer than they appear.*

They were approaching the turn onto Lower Dorset. Finn didn't have much time left. He decided to come out and say it.

"Are you even worried about Mom?"

Dad took a sharp breath. His knuckles became whiter as his hands gripped the steering wheel harder. "Yes, of course!"

"Then why are you doing work? Why aren't you trying to find her and get her to come home?"

"Leave it to me, Finn. Please."

"Has she called?"

"No . . . I'd tell you if she did."

"Then how do you even know she's okay?"

"Look," Dad sighed, clearly out of patience, "Gran says—"

Finn sat up straight. "Gran's heard from her?"

Dad shook his head. "No—no. She knows the way your Mom thinks. That's all."

"What did Gran say?"

"Finn, let's not do this now."

Normally, he'd keep pressing, but they were coming up to Gran's house. He let it drop. Maybe he'd get more out of her.

The tires rumbled on the gravel driveway. Finn instinctively glanced over at Dorset Peak's trailhead, behind Gran's house, to see if there were any cars parked on the road. There were none today.

"Good thing no one is up there," Dad said. His tone held that hopeful change-of-subject cheer that Finn knew all too well. "They say the storm tonight is going to be a big one. No one wants to be stuck on the mountain in that." Neither of them mentioned that it was Mom who'd started that habit of checking the trail. She was always concerned for the inexperienced hikers who might misjudge the weather or sunset.

Finn was pulling his stuff together when he realized Dad hadn't turned off the engine or made any move to exit the car.

"You're not even coming in?"

"No, I already told Gran on the phone. I have a long drive and I have to stay ahead of the storm." Finn was silent, and Dad finally met his gaze. "C'mon, Finn, don't look at me like that."

Finn grabbed his backpack and slammed the door as hard as he could. He wrestled his bike out of the trunk on his own. As he stomped up the walkway he heard the car pull out of the driveway. He didn't turn to wave right away and when he finally did, Dad was already down the road and out of sight. Everyone wanted to get away from him as fast as they could.

Finn stood for a moment surveying Gran's expansive yard. Even the trees looked tired of Vermont's extended summer. The air was humid. He hated this kind of weather. It felt as if all the oxygen had left the atmosphere. A cold front was supposed to arrive tonight. Finn couldn't wait.

He was reaching for the door when it opened from the inside—though only a few inches, just enough for Gran's wizened face to peek out. Her gray hair was uncharacteristically frizzing out in all directions, and Finn couldn't decide whether she hadn't slept in days or had just woken up.

"Finn! I'm not quite ready for you . . ." She looked behind her for a moment at a scene Finn could only guess at from his vantage point. "Um—I know! Why don't you bike over to Gabi's first and then come back here?"

"Gran, what's there to be ready for? It's only me." Finn put one hand on the door and started to step forward.

She slammed the door shut. He nearly fell backward down the slate steps.

"I'm sorry, Finn." Her voice came muffled from behind the thick wooden door. "Come back in an hour. Or two! Yes! Make it two!"

"Gran, are you okay?"

"Fine. Fine. Two hours, dear."

"What about your groceries?"

"Leave them on the steps. I'll get them. Thank you! Now go on, I'll be ready for you later."

Finn pressed his ear to the door and heard Gran

speaking in low tones. He had a fleeting thought that maybe he was ruining an early birthday surprise she'd planned for him, but that seemed unlikely. Finn had not had a real birthday party since he was three.

More likely, he'd interrupted a romantic interlude. He glanced back at the driveway and wondered if he'd somehow missed Doc Lovell's old Jeep, but there were no cars parked anywhere near the house. It was possible someone else had dropped Doc off, though. "So very disturbing," he muttered.

Gran and Doc Lovell had been dating for over two years, and while they liked to pretend they never stayed over at each other's houses, Finn knew better. He was happy Gran had someone. He just didn't want to think about it too much.

Still, it was unlike Gran to put anyone over her only grandson. Finn was used to top billing. It was a slight that stung.

"Okay, Gran," he shouted through the heavy wooden door. "I'll come back later. Text me if you need me." He waited a second to see if she'd change her mind. When it became painfully obvious she woudn't, he pulled out the small bag of groceries from the backpack and left it in front of her door. His questions for her would have to wait.

CHAPTER 2

Gabi's house reminded Finn of a giant acorn. It was like it had rolled down the side of the mountain and settled there, and someone had come along, hollowed it out and added windows. Gabi always complained about how small it was. Finn thought it was perfect. His own house was cavernous by comparison—always too empty, even before Mom left.

Gabi's mom was outside clipping the fading heads of late-summer flowers. She stood up and wiped the tips of her gardening gloves on her apron. Mrs. Rand didn't look a thing like Mom, but there was a familiarity in that gesture that reminded the hole inside Finn's chest to ache.

Mrs. Rand tipped back her sun hat and smiled warmly at him as he coasted up on his bike. "Good day to attack the weeds." She seemed completely in her element, and Finn found himself wondering why she and Mom hadn't become closer friends. They had so much in common, between the theater and gardening. Then again, Mom didn't have *any* close friends.

Mom even had a gardening hat like that. A memory nipped at the back of his brain and refused to be shooed away: Mom introducing him to her favorite garden dweller, the praying mantis.

"Did you know this is the only insect that can turn its heads 180 degrees to look at you over its shoulder? Sneaking up on a mantis is nearly impossible."

She'd urged him to try. He did and sure enough it spun around to look at him. He'd jumped backward, but Mom had smiled proudly at him just the same.

"See how she puts her eggs in this protective sac so they'll be safe all winter?" The branch near her held what looked like a brown Styrofoam walnut. Finn examined it closely. It was tiny.

"How will *she* stay safe?"

"Oh, well—she's not made to survive the winter."

The mantis didn't seem all that scary then. He felt bad for her and all her children who would grow up without her.

Of course, he learned much later that the females

sometimes cannibalized the males, which made him less inclined to sympathy.

Mrs. Rand broke his reverie. "Gabi's, uh—just gone down the road. You can probably catch her if you hurry."

Finn tried to find his smile. He wasn't quite sure what to say next. *Down the road* meant the old marble quarry, which had been filled in with water and opened to the public as a swimming hole. Dorset had been founded because of that marble quarry and the town was proud of it. But the Firths stopped going as a family years ago.

"I thought . . . she wasn't allowed." The older kids went on their own. Not them. They hung out in their own little world, grabbing day-old bagels from the Union Store on the green, or exploring the woods they knew so well.

"Gabi begged and I gave in." She said it hesitantly, fiddling with the gold necklace she always wore. "You're both getting older, aren't you? And today will probably be the last hot day of the season. Everyone trying to get in a bit more of summer." Mrs. Rand was talking brightly and too fast. She studied him for a second and Finn knew what was coming. Pity. "You could wait here for her if you like."

No. Today, he would reject this. Today, he would choose normal.

"That's okay, I'll catch up with Gabi. Thanks!" He pushed off on his bike.

She yelled after him, "Finn, are you sure? I made fresh lemonade!"

He kept going. The determination in his pedaling came easily because of what he was riding away from. He could practically hear Mrs. Rand's thoughts. *Poor family, been through so much, first the little girl, and now Liz leaving.* It wasn't until he was out of her line of sight that he realized what he was riding *toward.* His pace slowed. Normal was not something you could sail headlong into. He should know that by now.

He could see Gabi as he turned the corner onto Route 30. She was maybe fifty or sixty yards ahead. He watched her for a moment, debating what to do next. He could catch up and maybe convince her to go back home. That might work. Lemonade did sound good.

"Gabi!" Finn shouted.

She turned, saw Finn, and waved enthusiastically. He caught up and got off his bike to walk it alongside her.

"I thought you were supposed to be at Gran's," she said.

"Gran was real jumpy and sent me packing. I think Doc is over. Boyfriend visit."

Gabi raised an eyebrow at him. "We need to come up with a better term than girlfriend and boyfriend when talking about old people."

"Like what?"

"Beloved? Paramour?" Gabi gave him a sideways grin. "Boo?"

"You're going to make me lose my lunch." He was laughing. Gabi always got him to laugh. "I don't think any of those work. Nice try though."

"Since she's gonna be busy with her *boyfriend*"—she drew out the word in a mocking sing-song fashion that made Finn squirm—"Come with me!" She grabbed him by the wrist, her eyes wide with excitement. "The whole grade is going to be swimming at the quarry today and my mom actually said yes!"

Finn pulled back. "I'd, uh, I was kinda thinking we could hang out inside—"

"It's gorgeous out today! Tomorrow it will be fall and the day after that it will be winter. C'mon, please? Just for a little bit."

"It's gonna be full of tourists."

"It is not. Even if it is, we'll outnumber them. I'm not taking no for an answer!"

How could Gabi not know? It was true that he'd never told her any details. He had only said the word. *Drowned.* But the whole town knew everything about his family. And as much as he hated the gossip, it had also been his protection. It excused his weirdness, his quietness. People couldn't expect too much from him.

He'd assumed someone had told Gabi at some point. Sure, the Rands were flatlanders, not Dorset born, but Mrs. Rand obviously knew. Faith's death was local ghost lore now. Kids would talk about the little drowned girl who lived deep in the quarry water, how she'd grab you and pull you under to make you her playmate for eternity. Now it was painfully obvious that Gabi—who, when it came to regular life skills, always connected the dots before he did—had not put two and two together.

What he should've said was, *I can't go there. I can't swim in that water.*

What came out instead was, "Those guys hate me."

"No they don't. Stop worrying, you'll hang with me. It'll be fine. I promise."

Gabi was used to him being afraid of socializing. That was her strength, not his.

She began to walk on down the road and babble on about the weather. Finn wasn't listening; he was busy telling himself that he didn't have to actually go in the water. He could just sit on the rocks and read. Gabi would be happy with that. If he stayed focused on a book or an article, he could avoid thinking about where he was and soon enough it would be time to go. Maybe this was the first step toward fitting in.

"Earth to Finn!"

"Sorry, I was thinking."

"A million miles away as usual." She laughed. "Everyone from theater camp is going today."

"I don't want to hang out with them." Gabi didn't get it because for her, all that came naturally. She could make friends with anyone instantly. Finn had lived here his whole life and all he had was her.

"Do you remember the first day you met me at school?" she asked.

"Yeah . . ." Of course he did. It was the first day of third grade. She was the new kid from New York. The first thing she said when he introduced himself was "Wow, your parents like alliteration, don't they?"

To which he could only respond, "Huh?"

She asked him if he had brothers or sisters and he immediately answered yes. He never used the past tense. He was a twin. That's who he was. When he asked her in return she said, "One older brother." It wasn't until later he discovered that Xavier was also gone. He was a marine who had died overseas. Gabi's mother still wore a gold necklace with his name. Gabi's dad couldn't handle the grief. He'd left soon after Xavier died.

Finn had liked Gabi immediately, even if he sometimes needed a dictionary to understand her. When Gabi laughed, he couldn't help but laugh too. He remembered liking how she said the word "roof" wrong, like it was "ruff." He used to gleefully point it out to her, and she'd get angry. Back then she was a flatlander—an outsider to Dorset, and even though he'd been born here, so was he. He was a living reminder of a local tragedy. Someone to be whispered about.

"Do you know why we became friends?" Gabi asked him.

"Because I had the nerve to walk up and talk to you?" He figured this was a Gabi lesson to remind him to be social.

"Yeah, but what really did it was a few days later. I had a bad dream where you were in trouble. One of those dreams that felt so real I could remember every detail when I woke up. You were you, but not you.

You know how that sometimes happens in dreams?"

He nodded because in fact he did.

"You couldn't get back home and you couldn't see. So I sent you a big ball of sunlight and everything was all right."

"Magic sunlight, huh?"

"Don't make fun of me. It was third grade."

"Sounds like a flimsy basis for the start of a best friendship." He elbowed her in the arm playfully.

"Don't get all Mr. Skeptic on me. This is why I don't tell you anything."

"I'm sorry. It's cool. Though you do know sending me a ball of sunlight would usually make me run in the other direction."

"Well, today I'm bringing you to the sun, not vice versa. C'mon."

As they approached the small gravel parking lot, Finn's heart began to beat faster. The plan to hide inside a book seemed ridiculous now that he was faced with the reality. Seeing the big slabs of marble jutting out of the greenish water like giant, crooked grave markers made his stomach lurch. It had been a long time since he had been here, though he saw it often in dreams. The different levels of white rock and cliff face around the deep water made it look like a crooked mouth surrounded by rotting teeth. It was an almost perfect narrow rectangle, about the width of an Olympic swimming pool but much longer—and far deeper. It was no natural lake or water source. It was a wound sliced out of the mountain's base with unsettling precision, an ugly man-made thing, pretending to be nature.

But Gabi was wide-eyed and beaming like she had just entered one of her fantasy books. Finn parked his bike against the fence and followed her.

Hoping to remain inconspicuous, he pointed to a cluster of cut marble farthest from the water and closest to the parking lot. Gabi looked at him sideways but agreed with a smile. She pulled out some cheesy fashion magazines he had never seen her read before and laid out her towel. Finn sat down cross-legged on a large slab, while Gabi lay down on her stomach.

"It's so cool that this place exists." Her face was propped up in her hands, elbows on her towel.

Finn looked around, scanning faces for anyone who might be looking at him. Judging him for coming here.

"This couldn't happen back in New York. It's a wonder adults haven't come along and shut it down, gated it all up."

Finn often thought about that himself.

"It's like our own Stonehenge, only better!"

He could sort of imagine how it would be magical to her, with the way the giant marble slabs rose from the water, the way the surrounding trees seemed to grow straight from the rock.

"I like to pretend that this is part of Earthsea, you know?" She sighed the way she always did when she was about to talk about her fantasy books. At least she hasn't stopped reading those, Finn thought. He needed her to stay the Gabi he knew, his Gabi. The Gabi who loved the woods, the Gabi who'd searched for fairies and gnomes in the forest behind Gran's house. Life was so much simpler when they were in third grade.

"But you *don't* know," she said, pointing a finger at him in mock anger, "because you refuse to read my books! Someday you have to read Le Guin."

Usually, he would remind her how *she* refused to learn chess for him. But this time he was about to promise he would read them when he was cut off by the loud whooping of some boys jumping off the highest cliff into the deep water. It was a thirty-foot drop that only the bravest—or most reckless, depending on how you looked at it—chose to conquer. They took running leaps off the highest outcrop and did flips in midair. The sound of their bodies hitting the surface of the water struck Finn like a slap. He looked briefly at the greenish water and was sure it would swallow him whole. It would be a slow descent, eyes open, fingers splayed reaching for the ever diminishing sun—

"Gabi, this was a bad idea. I've gotta go."

"Come on, Finn, we just got here. You don't have to jump the cliffs. We don't even have to go in the water. What's the big deal anyway? You can sw—"

Gabi froze, looking wide-eyed at Finn.

"This isn't where . . .?"

Finn couldn't look her in the eye. He didn't even nod. He focused on the little cotton loops of thread in her towel.

"Oh Finn, why didn't you say anything?" She jumped up and began gathering her things.

Finn scrambled to his feet to get out of her way. He didn't want to meet her gaze. He should've told her. He had put her in an embarrassing situation by saying nothing.

Gabi began stumbling over words as she fought with her towel. "I'm so sorry. I always thought—I thought it was the lake. I thought the girl, the ghost girl—I thought it was a hundred-year-old story!"

She was doing her best to squash her unfolded beach towel into her small bag. Her face was bright red and she was avoiding looking at him.

"Hey, Gabi! Where you going?" A dripping wet Sebastian Connors materialized in front of them. Finn had done a good job of avoiding Sebastian so far. He was new, but he'd already become the leader of the boys who always took risks and never paid for them.

"Hi, Sebastian. I'm sorry, we have to go. I forgot—something," said Gabi.

"You just got here!" Sebastian trained an eye on Finn and smiled. "Are you making her leave before she even gets a toe in the water?"

And there it was, the moment when the alpha dog looked him in the eye and addressed him innocently enough. Somehow Finn was always awarded that chance. Maybe it was because of his height. It bought him a measure of respect before anyone got to know him. They always started by joking with him. There was that split second when Finn was treated the same as anyone else, and what he did next mattered. He could recognize the moment every time, only he could never tell what he was supposed to do or say to make the situation go in his favor.

The rest of Sebastian's crew began to assemble behind him, dripping wet and already full of adrenaline.

"It's my fault. I forgot something back at home," Finn offered.

Sebastian's eyes narrowed and his mouth turned up at one side. It had happened. Finn had somehow designated himself as prey.

"Well, no reason Gabi has to go then. Stay here with us. Let Finny head back on his own."

Finny. There were snickers from behind Sebastian now.

"No, no. We're both leaving." Gabi was still flustered.

"How about one jump before you go, Finny?" Sebastian was wielding a thick smile.

"No thanks. I really have to go."

"Have you ever even done it? You're not afraid, are you?" Sebastian nudged Troy Sprague. Troy and the rest began to shift uncomfortably, fearing where Sebastian was going to take this next.

"Thanks, but no." Finn bent to grab his bag.

"Why not? Afraid the ghost girl will drag you down to the bottom and keep you forever?" Sebastian snickered and looked at the others for affirmation. There was nothing but uncomfortable silence.

Gabi was staring daggers at Sebastian now and he was beginning to notice.

Troy leaned in and whispered something in Sebastian's ear. Finn watched the exchange and imagined the words. "Dude, that's his sister who drowned here." Sebastian's face contorted with confusion, then anger. It wasn't Finn who'd caused his embarrassment, but he knew that wouldn't matter. Guys like Sebastian were all the same. Whenever they embarrassed themselves, they would direct the blame elsewhere.

"C'mon, Finn, let's get out of here." Gabi's hand was suddenly in his. Finn watched Sebastian's eyes take in her gesture.

Finn could hear the fragments of whispers as they walked away, the word "sister," and then "mom." Sebastian practically shouted in Finn's direction, "Well, now I know why he's such a freak. That's messed up."

The words hit Finn from behind like a blow. It would've been easier if Sebastian had punched him. The truth was more painful.

ooo

Gabi walked double-time to keep pace with him till they reached her house. Mrs. Rand was no longer in sight and Finn was glad of it. He couldn't find it in himself to handle her sympathy and small talk now.

"We can go inside and get something to eat," she offered.

"No thanks, I'd better ride back to Gran's."

"Finn, I'm really sorry."

"It's not your fault."

"You shouldn't let what those idiots think bother you."

She sounded like Mom. Once while grocery shopping, when he was only seven or eight, he'd told Mom how some ladies were talking about her in the next aisle. He wanted her to be as angry as he was. Instead she'd said, "People are who they are. All you can control is how you treat them."

"You going to be okay?" Gabi asked.

Finn could only give her a nod and an affirmative grunt.

He rode away as she stood there in her front yard watching him. He didn't know how long she stayed there, because he didn't turn around.

I can tell you how long Gabi stayed there. I was watching. She waited, with her brows knitted in worry, till he was around the bend and completely out of sight. She walked slowly up to the house, her head and shoulders bowed with an invisible weight. Her small frame disappeared behind the door only to reappear in the picture window. She pulled out her phone and began to dial.

CHAPTER 3

The wind began to whip up as Finn sped down the road. It was that hot kind of wind that felt like the breath of a coming thunderstorm. Sure enough, clouds were starting to gather. Nighttime was arriving earlier and earlier now, but this was different. The sun should have still been high in the sky.

Finn could see the strip of clouds visible between the trees on either side of the road. Dark billows were blowing in fast, rolling over one another like gray mares in a race to see who could blot out the sun first. He'd seen something like it before, but it was in a movie, sped up on film.

Soon the thunder would be bouncing off the mountains and echoing through the town. Finn usually loved that, but today he just wanted to get inside and hide from everything.

One fat raindrop fell squarely on his head like an insult. He muttered curses he wasn't allowed to use. He fantasized that lightning would fry Sebastian and all of his crew in the quarry as they swam and then immediately felt guilty at the thought. He was angry at Dad and angry at Gran, too. None of this would have happened if Gran hadn't sent him away.

He dumped his bike behind Gran's garage and then sprinted up the driveway. She was framed in the doorway, waiting for him with a worried look on her face.

"Gabi called."

"Great. Just great." Finn pushed past her as she moved aside. "Don't worry. I won't be in your way."

He said it with too much anger and he knew it. Unable to face the pained look in her eyes, he raced up the stairs and down the hallway to the room that had always been his. He dumped his backpack on the floor and collapsed facedown on the bed.

There was a soft knock at the door.

"Finn, can we talk?"

Gran peeked in, and when he didn't protest she came and sat on the edge of the bed.

"Gabi told me what happened and I'm sorry. I know it's been hard for you. A lot harder than I realized."

Finn said nothing. He knew she meant well, but at the moment all he wanted to do was try to forget today had ever happened.

She lightly patted the small of his back. "Will's not coming by tonight, it's just us. How about I make you something to eat?"

Finn wanted to scoff that food wasn't the answer to all life's problems, but since he hadn't had anything to eat or drink for hours, his stomach betrayed him with a growl.

"I'll call you when it's ready." She smiled and left the room, closing the door quietly behind her. Her kindness in the face of his disrespect only made him feel worse.

He sat up, reached for his bag, and pulled out his tablet. The articles he'd downloaded ought to take his mind out of this world and into the grander universe. The great thing about spending time pondering space is that it's so big, it makes everything else feel small. It was probably why the other kids in school had no interest in it. There was nothing in their life they needed to make smaller.

He was wrong of course. You know that, don't you? Everyone has something they need to make smaller, more manageable. Everyone is wounded in some way.

It is what makes us human.

CHAPTER 4

The first glimpse of lightning flickered through the window, and Finn counted several seconds till he heard the far-off rumble of thunder.

He headed into the kitchen before Gran came to get him. That would be all she needed by way of an apology, but he intended on saying it anyway.

"I have some hot soup on. I've been waiting for this warm weather to end so I could enjoy a decent soup." She pulled out one of the wooden chairs for him and then moved back to the stove.

Finn sat and watched her as she ladled the thick soup into two bowls. It was his favorite, potato with big slabs of bacon.

"Here. Don't forget the bread." Gran handed him a dish that cradled a small homemade loaf. It was still hot. He ripped off the end and dipped it. The first bite felt warm all the way down as he swallowed.

"It's good?"

"It's always good, Gran. I'm sorry about before."

"Forget that. Eat."

As much as Finn hated to admit it, Dad had been right. This was what he needed. Gran's kitchen was still his safe place in this world. One smile from her could make everything seem better. She had a way of smiling that went right up to her eyes. He remembered how one Easter, right after Faith died, it was Gran who insisted that things should still happen normally for Finn. She led him by the hand around her big yard, helping him find the colorful plastic eggs that were barely hidden to begin with. His mother sat still, pale and quiet on the porch, Dad tending to her cautiously like she might break. Gran helped him count the eggs in his basket, laughing when he insisted he had eleventy. Finn reached up then, touched her cheeks, and said something about Gran's "crinkly eyes." Dad's head had spun toward him. "Finn! That's not nice." Gran had scoffed and told him to hush up, said Finn could point out her "crinkles" as much as he wanted. Finn loved them; they were the beautiful lines that only appeared for him. Back then, smiles were hard-won in his family.

Come to think of it, it wasn't much different now.

He left the spoon in the bowl and took a deep breath, steadying himself. "Gran, I need to know why Mom left."

If she was surprised to get the question, her face didn't show it. Searching her gray eyes, he pressed on. "Does she have a boyfriend? Is she leaving Dad?" *And me.* The more he thought about what was going on, the more he landed on divorce as the most obvious answer. Occam's Razor: simpler theories are always the best ones. He had heard them arguing for weeks, after all. Mom was probably out building a new life somewhere.

"Oh no, it's nothing like that!" Gran's face hardened the way it did when she became fed up with someone in town. "Who told you that?"

"Gran, no one has told me anything!"

She took off her apron, tossing it on the opposite chair, and sat down next to him. "Haven't you asked your father about this?"

"Yes, but he just keeps saying she'll be back soon." He parroted his father's detached professorial speech: "She just needs some time."

"Oh, I see." For a moment, she seemed unguarded. Finn could tell she was thinking hard. "Well, in large part, I believe that to be true."

"Gran, does she call you? Has she said anything—about me?"

She looked pained. "No. She has not. And it wouldn't be fair to your father for me to conjecture and feed you ideas."

Finn's imagination began to move into dark places. Mom's constant migraines. How they'd kept her in bed during so many events: his kindergarten graduation, the endless school pageants, even the science fair. They all had something in common. They were rites of passage, rites that Faith should have been doing along with him.

"You know something and you won't tell me."

"That's not what I said."

"Gran!"

She stared at the blank wall as if it were suddenly a picture window only she could see out. "Your father has to be the one to explain this to you, Finn. I can't, I'm sorry."

Finn sighed and dropped the heel of the bread into his soup bowl. His father was miles away, yet he somehow managed to also be here, roadblocking him again.

"Have some more soup. I'm going to tell you a

story about our family."

"I don't want to hear any ancient stories, Gran. I want to hear about now."

She studied him for a moment, her eyes narrowed. "Everything is now, dear boy. And make no mistake, things that happened before you were born have everything to do with who you are and what you do. So much of our lives are built on what happened before we even arrived. *The past is never dead. It's not even past.* Faulkner said that."

She paused, looking for some sort of reaction from Finn. He nodded with a mouthful of soup. It all sounded like one of Dad's pretentious lectures about why history was as important as science. He resigned himself to hearing her out. Maybe she'd loop back around to talking about Mom when she was ready.

"You know, I've never gotten along with my sisters."

Finn rolled his eyes in frustration. He had no interest in listening to her complain about Aunt Ev and Aunt Billie.

"Trust me. This is as good a place to start as any." The rain was thudding against the skylight now like it was knocking and asking to be let in.

"Ev and Billie have been thorns in my side for

years." Gran laughed a little at this like it was a joke, but it was a sad sort of laugh. "Sisters should be close. I wish we were closer."

"I always thought you got along okay with Aunt Ev." He reached for the bread loaf once more. This conversation was no longer his as far as he was concerned; he might as well dig in and eat.

"Oh, we coexist. So little in common though. She's impulsive and that makes it hard for us to work together. You see, we've had . . . long-standing family responsibilities." She looked again at that invisible picture window, then focused back on him. "Still, Ev's always been much easier to manage than Billie."

There was a sudden crash out on the deck and Finn instinctively jumped up in front of Gran. She stood up and brushed by him to look out the window. "It's all right. Only the storm taking down a rotted branch. It's hit the deck, but there's no damage."

"I can take care of it for you tomorrow. Cut it up for kindling."

Gran smiled. "You're a big help to me. You know that, right?"

Finn looked away. He shouldn't have complained about spending the weekend. "I could help more," he said.

She sat down again, but this time in the chair closest to the big cast iron oven. "You do enough. Now, anyway, I was telling you about the three of us. We were the Sykes sisters. Our neighbors lumped us together whether we liked it or not. It's a small town now—it was even smaller then. Everyone knew everyone else's business."

"They still do."

"Even more so then, if you can believe it. It was a different time for young women of course. We didn't have the opportunities that are available now. Our parents hoped we'd stay on the farm till it was time to marry. Ideally, they'd have final approval of each groom and we'd all live in town and produce many grandchildren for Dad to bounce on his knee."

Finn wasn't sure if her tone was one of mocking or remorse. Gran was the only sister to have married and she only had one daughter, his mother. And right now Mom was who he cared about. This little story was Gran's way of evading his questions.

"Gran—"

"It may not surprise you," she went on, talking over him, "to know that I didn't much like that plan and neither did Evelyn. I did not intend on wasting the brain God had given me. I was going off to school as soon as possible. Ev intended on getting a train out of Dorset even if it meant jumping a boxcar."

Now that caught his attention. "You're kidding, right?" He tried to picture short, stout Aunt Ev trying to hop onto a moving train. He couldn't imagine any of them ever being young, as hard as he tried.

"Nope. She would've done it, too. As for Billie, well, she was just fine with staying in Dorset. Her plan was to marry the most eligible bachelor in town. The problem was, the bachelor was the type of spoiled rich boy who didn't believe in planning for anything. He knew he was going to inherit his father's land and didn't need to study or work hard. And he was handsome on top of all that, the kind of boy who'd make girls stand a little taller as soon as he entered the room. Naturally, I had no patience for him."

The guy with everything. Finn hated him already.

"None of his outward charms worked on me, not his pale gray eyes, square jaw," she reached over and with her thumb and forefinger pinched a section of Finn's unruly hair and then let it go, "shiny auburn hair."

Finn's hand held the last spoonful of his soup in mid-air.

She sat back and smiled at him. "That's right. Your grandfather, my Jack. You do look just like him, Finn. It's uncanny. I stayed in Dorset after all."

It wasn't the first time Finn heard that he was the spitting image of Grandpa Jack. Only it was the first time he had heard Grandpa Jack described as handsome. The Grandpa Jack he remembered was frail and hunched over. If girls loved him, he certainly had something that Finn didn't. All the girls except—

"Wait! You didn't like him! You said—"

"Well, Dorset suffered three straight years of drought. His family's farm fared badly. The stress of it all took Jack's father, most likely a heart attack. Your grandfather ended up running the farm. Adversity brings out the true character in people. Remember that, Finn. Jack grew into someone I admired, someone I came to love very much."

"And Aunt Billie never forgave you?"

"I suppose not. Aunt Ev was quite furious with me, too."

"But why?"

"Because I didn't want to leave Dorset after all. We had always talked about doing grand things together and suddenly all I wanted was right here."

"But Aunt Ev didn't move away!"

"Oh, she did. She just came back. We all come back."

He was about to ask why, but she didn't give him a chance.

"Billie became increasingly bitter. She grew quiet and no longer went out with friends. She spent most of her free time writing in mysterious notebooks that she wouldn't let any of us see. One Sunday morning I pretended to be ill, and when the others left for church I sneaked into her room, found the loose floorboard that functioned as her hiding spot, and read them."

Finn thought that was a pretty nasty thing for Gran to do to her sister, but realized he was now on the edge of his seat. "What did they say?"

"They were notes, incredibly detailed notes about *my* life. About Jack and me, where we met, how we met, the first time we were alone together. Or at least, I thought we were alone together."

"So she was stalking you guys? That's creepy."

"You can say that. She appeared to be taking notes in an effort to figure out where she went wrong. As if there were a way she could go back and fix it. She was looking for a path to a world in which she and Jack were together."

"Huh." Finn didn't much care for tales of lovelorn teenagers, but this part intrigued him—and reminded him of an article he'd been reading earlier. "Sounds like she was looking for a parallel universe. There's a new quantum theory in physics about them, you know. It's based on the Many Worlds principle, but surprisingly different."

Gran was looking at him the way Gabi did before she would tell him to stop, back up, and define the three terms in the last sentence. Finn knew when to submit. "Okay, so you know about the Many Worlds theory?"

"Yes," she said cautiously. "I think so."

Finn was used to people pretending to understand him when he talked science; he would make this simple. "The idea is that we exist in a multiverse. That there are other universes pushed up right next to us, almost identical to ours but with small changes."

"A whole universe, next to ours?"

"Yeah, it's a weird thing to wrap your head around." He swallowed another spoonful of soup. "They would be worlds similar to our own, with minor changes. It's like Chaos Theory in a way. You've heard of the Butterfly Effect?"

"Yes. I think so. It's about small changes being able to effect things a world away?"

"Right! Something as simple as the beat of a butterfly wing in Mexico"—he held his now empty spoon up in the air like it was flying—"can make a hurricane happen in China, or in this case, make Grandpa Jack marry someone else." Finn laughed, expecting Gran to laugh with him. She just stared and waited, so he kept going. "Anyway, all those little butterfly wing beats create new universes! Amazing, right?"

She didn't look amazed; she looked scared. "So this is the new theory?"

"No, that's the *old* one. The *new* part is something really cool. It's nowhere near mathematically proven, but it's also no longer out of the realm of possibility. It's called MIW—the Many *Interacting* Worlds Theory. It's where universes that exist next to each other actually interact on the quantum level." Finn reached for another slice of warm bread from the bowl in the center of the table. Gran grabbed his wrist and held it tight, stopping him.

"Wait! How would they interact?"

"Oh, this is all theory, Gran. But a lot of weird stuff happens in quantum mechanics, things that shouldn't, like light behaving both as a particle and a wave. These scientists who did the study say that this may be the reason for all the quantum weirdness, parallel universes interacting," he clapped his hands together loudly, "smashing into each other. Neat, huh?"

"*How*? How do they smash into each other? Can someone hop to another universe?" Her eyes grew wide and Finn thought she looked a little panicked.

"This is all on the quantum level, Gran. They're talking about particles, not people."

"How do they know that? They don't really know anything, do they?" She stood up from the table, grabbing a dishtowel off the counter and wiping her hands on it before mindlessly throwing it into the trash.

"Gran, it's not about human beings."

She was looking past him now, her mind miles away. There was an uncomfortable silence until she said, "All it takes is one little bend, and two parallel lines are no longer parallel."

Now Finn was confused. "Well, yeah, that's mathematically true—"

"I'm not feeling well, Finn. I'm going to bed. Can you clean up for me?" She began to shuffle to the doorway. "It's one of my . . . headaches."

Finn hoped it wouldn't be like Mom's. He'd have to call Doc to drive her to the ER in Rutland.

"Is it going to be a bad one?" he asked.

"If I don't rest it could get worse."

Her voice trailed off as she left the room and walked down the hallway, leaving Finn alone in the kitchen with the sounds of the ticking clock and the rain. He rose from his chair and began clearing the dishes. He rescued the dishtowel from the trashcan and put the leftover soup in the fridge.

He paused in front of his bedroom door with one hand on the doorknob, listening. There were no sounds coming from her room down the hall. She must already be lying down. He hoped she would be able to rest.

What he planned to do next would be easier once she was sound asleep.

CHAPTER 5

Finn had already searched his own house top to bottom—except for Dad's office, because if so much as a paper clip was out of place, Dad would know. His investigation had yielded no clues about Mom's whereabouts: no scraps of paper with cryptic information, no letters, no emails, not one hint about where she could have gone.

But Mom never went anywhere without sending Gran a postcard. It was an old-fashioned habit that Finn found silly when she could just text her a photo. Gran's house might have exactly what he was looking for.

She clearly knew more than she was letting on.

Late that night Finn pried open his bedroom door and moved slowly down the dark hallway, aware of his heart beating in his chest. Was the house that quiet? Maybe it was actually the grandmother clock on the landing ticking loudly. *"It's called a grandmother and not a grandfather because the door isn't a glass panel. All the mysterious doodads and gears are hidden inside on a grandmother clock."* That's what Gran said about it whenever anyone asked. Usually Finn didn't even notice the ticking. Now it was the loudest noise in the house.

He went first to the dining room. The china cabinet was jam-packed with linens, papers, candles, a 1970s fondue set, a large number of collectible thimbles, and some old records. He pushed through to the papers, but they were only old tax forms. No recent credit card statements or postcards, nothing that would give him a clue as to where Mom went.

The living room, with its overstuffed chairs and gigantic fireplace, usually made him feel warm and comfortable, only now in the dark the fireplace looked like a gaping black hole and the chairs were sagging under its pull. He looked around, but there was nothing in here that could hide a stash of letters. That left one more place. The basement.

No one went down there anymore. The stairs had been deemed too dangerous for Gran three years ago. His parents had her laundry machines moved up to the mudroom. When Finn was younger, Gran used to stock food down there and send him for evaporated milk or canned peaches. He'd always tried to be brave about it, but the basement was dark and full of wolf spiders. Those things were tarantula-huge.

He couldn't imagine what horrors it hid now, when no one even opened this door. He gently moved the hook off its metal eye to unbolt it. The door immediately sighed open as if it had been straining forever against that one little piece of metal.

It took a moment for his eyes to register anything in the darkness below. The familiar childhood smells of dust, mold, and wood met him before anything he could see. He turned on his cell phone flashlight and saw the familiar red slatted stairs. He reached for the light switch and realized it was already in the on position. Bulb out. He walked slowly down the rickety stairs, testing each one to make sure it wasn't rotted through. They made an awful racket; he took them one by one, listening for movement above.

When he got to the bottom he was surprised to find the basement hadn't turned into a spider-infested mummy's tomb after all. Grandpa Jack's woodworking table was still standing up against the far wall. Solid and made of oak, it looked like it was also holding up the side of the house. Gran had kept it like a shrine to him after he passed. Finn could still picture him sitting there, unrolling his canvas to reveal tools that looked capable of an archaeological dig.

Finn picked up a copy of a woodworking magazine from 2002 and found something catching the light below it. Gran's blue wristwatch. The one she fretted over last year because she thought she'd lost it in town. She was sure the clasp had come undone and it was gone forever. He was at once thrilled to have found it for her and disappointed he had no way of returning it without admitting he was a snoop. Though hadn't she admitted to doing the same exact thing with Aunt Billie? Maybe she would understand . . . or maybe not.

He pocketed the watch anyway. He'd put it someplace she was bound to find it.

Finn continued to the back of the basement, winding his way through cardboard boxes full of seasonal decorations that required too much effort to dig out of storage anymore. He was stopped short by a colorful plastic teeter-totter. It was covered in cobwebs now, its colors hidden by years of layered dust, but Finn knew them anyway. Blue and green and vibrant yellow. His brain yielded a perfect memory:

him and Faith in Gran's backyard on this little piece of plastic made for the weight of two toddlers.

"You were relegated to the basement afterwards, weren't you?" he whispered to it as if it was a sad sentient being that missed its sole purpose.

Behind it rested a stroller, the double kind made for twins. His grandparents had kept these memories in their basement, unwilling to toss them away or donate them, hiding them like an internal injury. He had come looking for clues about Mom and found only Faith.

He decided to give up on the basement. Gran couldn't have hidden anything here, not without someone's help, and frankly the whole thing was beginning to make him feel like a creep.

He was halfway up the slatted stairs again when he noticed something stuffed between the fourth and fifth stair, only visible from this angle. He pulled it free. It was a black trash bag, knotted against itself at the top. Finn sat on the stair with it in front of him.

He found himself afraid to see what was inside. Cautiously, he opened it.

First, he spied the familiar floral pattern of his mother's overnight bag. He unzipped it and inside, on top of a pile of clothing, he saw his mother's wallet and purse and phone. It looked as if someone had packed her things in a hurry, all her important things.

All her everyday possessions were in his hands. He reached in and picked up the purse he wished he could still see hanging off the back of the kitchen chair every night. It had only been a few weeks since Mom left, but he felt as if he were holding ancient relics, as if these objects should be in a museum and only handled with white gloves. He opened the wallet and looked at his mother's driver's license through the little clear plastic pocket. Her signature was below the smiling photo, the familiar handwriting he missed so much and kept waiting to find in the mailbox each day. His fingers lingered over the signature as if touching it could somehow summon the signer.

And the phone. Battery dead.

A small bass drum began to beat in his chest. These were things she would've needed the last three weeks.

Things she would've taken with her.

He raced up the stairs. No longer concerned about noise, he shouted, "Gran!"

How could she hide this from him? He stumbled across the threshold and didn't bother to close it or bolt the door. He had every right to snoop! She had to give him answers now.

"Gran!" he yelled down the hall. He had made enough noise to wake the dead. Still there was no sound on the other side of her door.

"Gran?"

He knocked loudly. Still no answer.

Suddenly, someone grabbed his shoulder. He spun around to find Gran standing where she hadn't been two seconds before.

CHAPTER 6

"Gran! You scared me." He steadied himself against the opposite wall with his left hand, then held up the bag in his right like an accusation. "Why do you have this? Tell me. Now!"

He expected his tone to shock her. Instead she gently nodded and said, "We need to talk. Let's go to the living room."

She sat on the overstuffed sofa and patted the cushion next to her. It was more of an order than an invite. He took a seat. It was still dark, due to both the early hour and the cloud cover from last night's storm. Finn went to turn on the lamp on the side table. She grabbed his arm in mid-reach and shook her head no.

"I know you're angry. But you need to listen now." She was staring at him. Taking him in like she had never seen him before. It was very disconcerting. "I have something I need to tell you."

"Yes, you do! Why do you have Mom's things?"

She grasped both his hands and leaned in with an intensity that completely unnerved him. Finn saw flecks of gold in the blue of her eyes and wondered why he never noticed them before.

"I've planned this conversation over and over in my mind since the day you were born. I imagined it would be Liz and me talking to you together and—" She shook her head sadly and Finn heard the wind whistle through the cold fireplace behind him.

"Where is she?" Finn's entire nervous system froze with hope and fear. Everything hinged on Gran's answer.

"It's a bit more complicated than *where*."

"Is she—okay?"

Gran pulled him in for a fierce hug. Her arms were strong, like they felt after he fell off his bike when he was little. She pushed him away to arm's length while still holding firmly onto his shoulders.

"She loves you. We both do. More than you can imagine."

"You're scaring me." Finn surprised himself with how small his voice sounded.

"Oh, I don't want to scare you!" She wrung her hands together nervously. Finn had never seen her like this. "I'm not supposed to scare you. Well, maybe I am. I don't know! She didn't really give me much to go on. Let's say for expediency's sake that it's okay to be scared." She eyed the clock on the cable box over the TV and frowned.

"The message I have for you is not from your mother. It's from—well—me. The future me, to be exact. I am the Gran you knew several years ago. How old are you now? No—wait!" She pushed her palm up toward his face so quickly she nearly hit him in the nose. "Don't tell me. I don't want to know. Sorry about that." She patted his cheek as if that would somehow realign his features. "Well, *your* Gran and I, we are sort of working together on this." She shot a sad, worried glance down the hallway before she focused back on his face once more. "The Gran you know, she asked me to come forward and do this."

It took him a moment to register each word. There was no logic he could follow. She wasn't joking. Her voice had a seriousness in it he had never heard before, and it made his body respond with a small involuntary shudder.

"That doesn't make any sense. Are you feeling okay, Gran?"

"I know this is hard to comprehend. Try and think of me as one of your equations. Yes, that will do! Let's see, now don't tell me your exact age. Please. I'm going to guess it's only about five years, though. Think of me as Gran Minus Five. That's good, isn't it?" She placed a hand over his—and that's when Finn saw the watch.

She was wearing the slim blue watch!

"How did you find that?" He pointed at her wrist and then immediately shoved his hand into his pocket. It was empty! It was like a magic trick. "You said you lost it! I just found it downstairs on Grandpa's table—"

"Oh, well, now that you've told me, I haven't lost it, have I? Now listen carefully and promise not to interrupt till I'm done."

She was staring straight into his eyes and waiting for him to agree before she continued. Finn forced his head into a quick nod.

She took a deep breath. "I have died. Last night, I passed away in my sleep."

"That's not funny, Gran!" He involuntarily looked down the hallway toward her bedroom, then back at her. Whatever game she was playing, he didn't like it one bit.

"I'm not trying to be funny and now you're interrupting."

Her short-cropped hair had too many shades of silver and gray to count, and she smelled like peppermint. Everything about her was the way Gran always was, but something *was* off. Something besides the watch trick. Finn could not deny that she didn't seem to be the same Gran as last night.

Gran was getting older and perhaps this was the beginning of a decline. Dementia. It was entirely possible that he and Dad had missed the signs.

"Did you ever wonder why your mother loves history so much?" asked Gran.

"I don't know, because she married a history professor?" This came out ruder than he expected.

She let out a disappointed sigh, but it was directed at herself, not him. She admonished herself with a whispered, "The beginning, Beth." Then she inhaled sharply, closed her eyes, and said, "Your mother is what we call a Traveler. She can cross the folds of time. She can travel to the past and the future."

Finn instantly felt all alone. Gran had lost her mind. His face must have registered his horror.

"Now don't look at me like that! I'm perfectly sane. Your mother is a Traveler. I am a Traveler and so are your aunts. It runs on the female side of the bloodline."

She looked at the clock again, then the watch.

It was outrageous. He'd have to call Doc, tell him Gran wasn't lucid. "You're saying that all the women in my family can time travel?"

"Well, don't be ridiculous." She lifted her chin and straightened her shoulders. "Only on your mother's side." She said it as if Dad's side were somehow deficient.

"Gran, please." He took a last desperate shot at appealing to whatever reason she had left. "Why would our family be the only one in the world that could do that?"

"Who said anything about being the only ones? There have been many signs we're not alone. We just happen to be the only ones in Dorset. And that's why it's up to us to find your mother."

He remembered the bag. In his shock he had let it drop to the floor. He picked it up and brandished it at her. "How—why?!"

"They packed that up the day she disappeared. It had to look as if she'd moved out. *Your* Gran and your dad, they didn't want you—or the police—to think she had come to any harm."

"Gran! You told me she was okay!" The words rushed out all at once and it felt as if his last breath went with them.

"*Your* Gran told me they needed everyone to think she left of her own accord." Her eyes were wet. She hadn't answered his question.

"Gran—! She—she's not . . ."

She turned her head away. "We are all alive or dead at some point." She looked back at him and put her hand resassuringly on his knee. "But she didn't leave you, Finn. They're trying to figure out *when* she is. Your father is tirelessly searching for clues."

He had tried to grasp what she was getting at. "She's lost?"

"We think so. We knew it would be risky. We didn't want her to go. They—I mean *we*, that is, the me from your time, and your father—have been trying to talk her out of the last jump for over a year. She wouldn't listen. She said she knew what was best. And she *is* the best Traveler in our family. Each generation surpasses the previous one."

Almost all respected physicists still considered time travel an impossibility. This he knew. Still, his heart asked the next question without his brain's permission. "So then can I"—he fidgeted in the chair—"um, time travel?" It was an absurd question and he couldn't believe he was asking it.

"No. No man in our family has ever been able to Travel," she said gently. She was still monitoring both the clock over the television and her wristwatch as if something big was about to happen. "But there is another possibility. Your mother built a portal, a way to reach her in case of this kind of emergency."

Portal. That was a word Gabi loved. It was the kind of word one of her favorite fantasy books would use. Finn's science books talked about wormholes, not portals.

"It's in a tree," Gran went on. "A tree rooted to more than the earth. It stands outside the laws of time, an anchor of sorts, letting people travel from node to node—point to point along the timeline. She made it in case of this kind of emergency."

"A tree? She built a tree?"

"No, the tree grew as trees normally do! Listen! She *turned* it *into* a portal. It's amazing—none of us have managed anything like that before. She's certainly the most talented Traveler we've ever had." She was beaming, proud of her daughter. "The tree is a secret. No one knows about it but your mother and me, not even your father."

"So—she made it for me?"

Gran shifted uncomfortably for a moment and looked away. "It was a fail-safe she made back years ago. In case she got lost. A shortcut, so to speak, a line directly to her."

"So, she made it for *you*?"

"No. Not for me." She looked out the window up toward Dorset Peak.

"Well, who did she make it— "

Finn stopped himself in midsentence. She made it for Faith. For her only daughter, the next time traveler.

Gran's voice took on the brightness of someone who was hiding a darker truth. "We still think it might work for you. It's an outside chance, but it's all we have."

"Work for me? You mean let me get to Mom wherever she is?"

"*When*ever."

"Why me, though? Why haven't *you* tried to use it?"

"I may have tried. I mean, maybe I do try. I don't know. I only know that whatever your mother and

Future Me attempt, it doesn't work. Now, this is your task."

He should call Doc and have him take her to the hospital in Rutland. That would be the responsible thing to do. Only the idea that he, the useless remainder, could possibly help bring back Mom made him keep asking her questions.

"What happens if it doesn't work for me? What then?"

"We don't need to go into that."

"Yes, we do. Tell me."

"Well, maybe nothing. It would just be a regular old tree to you."

"Or? There's more. You're hiding something. I can always tell when you're hiding something."

She began to examine the arm of the sofa. "You could get stuck somewhere, or lost entirely."

Finn brought her gaze back to him by placing his hand over hers. "What does that mean, 'lost entirely?'"

"You could be obliterated—sliced clear through on a cellular level. You could die."

"That's insane! Why would you want me to even try?" He caught himself, reminded himself that this was all ridiculous, impossible.

"You're all we have now, Finn. It may not have been made with you in mind, but still, we have to try. You are a twin. There's never been a set of twins in our family before. Maybe—just maybe something rubbed off on you in the womb."

Finn was tempted to remind her that he and Faith were *fraternal* twins—no more genetically similar than any other pair of siblings. But he immediately saw the absurdity of bringing science into this conversation.

Gran pointed toward the window. "The portal is on top of Dorset Peak. It might help you find her."

Find her. The words made something inside him stir. Wasn't that what he'd been wanting? Someone to find her. He had screamed the same words in anger at his father only a few weeks ago: "*Go, find her!*" Now, he could do it himself. Sure, the idea of a portal was pure fantasy, but maybe there was a real clue there, a note or something. He had to keep Gran talking, even if it meant entertaining an idea that was wholly unscientific.

"Is there a map?"

"She said you wouldn't need one. You'll find it."

"How am I supposed to find one particular tree on an entire mountain?"

"I don't know, but I know Future Me thinks you can."

Finn remembered how much Mom loved hiking. How Dorset Peak was her favorite trail because the leaf peepers mostly left it alone. She knew that trail better than anyone.

He was trying to fit all the pieces together in his brain, but his rational side kept whispering, *Gran is sick. You need to get her help.*

Gran leaned in like they were conspirators. "This is what is going to happen next. Doc Lovell is on his way over to check on me. He's a good man. You do as he says, you can trust him."

Finn wondered for a moment if she knew that she was dating him, that he had become her boyfriend. Of course she knew! This was insane; she wasn't from the past. But she had just called him Doc Lovell. She never called him anything but Will anymore.

"Go meet him in the driveway and act as if you're just arriving. Tell him your father waited till the storm let up a bit before he left town. That he just dropped you off. You haven't spoken with me at all today, do you understand?" She jumped up from the sofa, clearly expecting him to follow her.

"No. I don't understand. I don't understand any of this!"

"I'll explain more later. It must seem like I won't have the time, but I will, you'll see." She ducked down the hallway and brought back his sneakers and backpack from the guest room, thrusting them at him. She waited impatiently for him to get his shoes on and pulled him by the wrist to the top of the staircase while he was still hopping on one foot.

"Go back to the driveway and wait. Don't come back inside unless you're with Doc Lovell, okay?" He numbly followed her down the stairs to the door. With her hand on the knob, she stopped and looked up at him. Finn watched her lips form a small, sad smile. She rested the palm of her free hand against his cheek. Her eyes were brighter than usual. Were there fewer crinkles? That couldn't be possible.

"You're so grown up already. You'll have to grow up even faster from here on out, I imagine."

"I don't want to be a grown-up," he said. Right now, he wasn't even sure he wanted to be Finn. It was good that Doc was coming. He would help. He'd fix this. He'd get her medications switched, and everything would be okay. They'd laugh about this in a few days.

"None of us ever want to grow up, but the alternative isn't any prettier." Gran's eyes were brimming with tears. "I want you to know I don't regret anything. I love you, Finn."

"I—I love you too, Gran." He had no idea what she meant about regret.

This was impossible; she was hopelessly confused. He'd use the scientific method to set her straight. A hypothesis was already constructed for him: *The women in his family could time travel.* It was up to him to disprove it. He never defied her, but she wasn't herself.

He darted by her as fast as he could, bounding up the stairs two by two, bolting down the hallway.

"Finn! No!"

It was the smell that hit him first. Pungent and sour, as though someone had been ill. Lying in the bed was Gran. Only it couldn't be, because she was coming up behind him as well, breathing fast after chasing him down the hall. He looked at the bed and back to her. Same person, one alive and one dead.

"I—I didn't want you to see me like this," she stammered.

Finn staggered back from her and held on to the dresser for support. He realized that brought him closer to the body in the bed so he jumped forward.

It was Gran all right. She was lying on her back and her eyes were open, only they were seeing nothing. Everything else in the room was horribly, frustratingly normal. Her stack of paperbacks on the nightstand. Her pill organizer. Her pink slippers neatly placed next to the bed. This room wasn't supposed to contain a lifeless Gran. You could almost be fooled. Almost.

He tried to make his mouth say something. Nothing came out. Then came the sound of tires on gravel, and Gran, the one who was alive, looked down the hallway and back at him.

"We'll have to leave through the back door now. Oh Finn, I tried to spare you this!"

She forcefully led him down the hall. Too stunned to do anything but go along, he stumbled after her. Gran opened the door and went out first, pulling him behind her with that strength she hadn't displayed in years.

"You'll see me again. You will. Don't be sad. I love you so."

He stumbled a few feet in the wet mud before his knees gave out completely. Sliding to the grass, he rested his head against the siding of the house. He opened his eyes and found his voice. "How, Gran?

How can this be real?"

Finn waited for a response, but he would have to keep waiting. Because Gran was gone. He was all alone.

He heard Doc Lovell's voice calling her name cheerfully as he came inside. "Beth? I hope you made biscuits!"

Finn couldn't see him from outside. He only heard him move through the house, but he could picture him clearly. Doc always looked exactly the same. His white hair was perfectly combed. He always wore the same kind of starched, plaid, button-up shirt, neatly tucked into baggy, wrinkled pants, with mud-covered sneakers. Gran teased Doc all the time, saying people were only supposed to look at his second floor because his foundation was a mess.

Finn heard Doc say her name again, sounding as confused as Finn had been earlier. Then it echoed much more cautiously: "Beth?" and finally, an anguished yell. Finn heard it with his heart.

He tried to get up, but he stumbled. The smell was still with him; it was in his mouth. Death had a taste. He threw up in the bushes, stood shakily, and wiped his hands on his jeans. He felt a crinkle in his pocket and stuck his hand inside—Gran's list. An hour ago it was only a shopping list, but now it was another relic.

He opened it up. It looked different, smudged through with a dark ink that had bled from the other side. The handwriting was scrawled as if done quickly, but it was definitely Gran's. He turned it over and read:

I was wrong. Don't trust anyone.

CHAPTER 7

Finn edged around the side of the house, doing his best to not make any noise. The wind picked up and he heard fat drops of rain, spaced far apart, thudding against the hard ground. All of his senses were magnified. It was an uncomfortable sort of internal buzzing that he couldn't stop. His skin vibrated with it. He heard a vole rustle through the leaves and at the same time he heard Doc Lovell on the phone inside. Doc spoke urgently. Finn couldn't make out individual words.

There was still one message he could hear loud and clear; it echoed in his brain even though he had only read the words.

Don't trust anyone.

Leaning against the siding, he clumsily tied his muddied shoelaces. He couldn't go to Doc for help.

The plan was altered. Gran had changed her mind about him. *Anyone.*

Finn looked over at the trailhead, and the mountain didn't look protective. It looked like a three-thousand-foot wall he had to climb to get to Mom. If he even could get to her.

He needed help.

Anyone. Gran couldn't possibly have meant Gabi.

There was nowhere else to go. He had trusted Gabi since the third grade and no matter what the note said, he needed someone on his side right now.

Running through the back woods and out of sight of the main road, he clutched his backpack straps tight and took off through the trees. Branches fell around him as the wind kicked up, and another low rumble of thunder echoed through the valley. The line of thunderstorms was still coming. Even though he knew it was dangerous to remain in the woods, he stayed inside the tree line. He didn't want Doc to find him on the road.

His breathing became ragged with the running, or maybe it was the remembering.

This couldn't be happening. Gran couldn't be dead.

The repetition of one hard footfall after another helped dull the constant buzzing. He could think a little more clearly. Gran had been there. She had been in bed *and* standing behind him at the same time. That was impossible. The only explanation was that Gran, or more accurately, Gran -5, was telling the truth.

Maybe Gabi had been right all along; maybe her fantasy novels went beyond his science textbooks.

No! He was not ready to concede that science had it wrong. How could all the women in his family time travel?

Vague images of biology homework flashed in his brain, Punnett squares and mitochondrial DNA. Certain traits *were* only hereditary through the female line. He remembered reading that it was possible for a gene to go from only mother to daughter through generations. Science didn't have to be *wrong*. Science could explain anything given enough time.

A huge clap of thunder hit the sky like a punch, reverberating in his chest.

He began moving faster, leaping over fallen branches. His toe caught on a root and he went sprawling, catching himself right before he would've smashed his face against a large rock. He lay there on his stomach for a moment, catching his breath and contemplating his mortality.

He recognized the smell in his nostrils. Ozone. Another flash of lightning lit up the sky like the world itself was cracking in half. Close. Too close.

He stood up and found he couldn't decide which way to point his feet. Neither of his choices were good: stay in the woods where he could be hit by lightning, or move out onto the road where he could be spotted.

Don't trust anyone.

That meant he was supposed to do this on his own. But that wasn't who he was. He was the one who studied, analyzed, found answers. He didn't hike mountains and find portals. "Portals!" He said the word aloud in disbelief. And what would happen if he found it? He couldn't time travel. He'd be obliterated—how did Gran -5 put it again? "Sliced clear through on the cellular level"?

No, that could not be. If there was a tree, that was all it was. A tree. There was no such thing as time travel! His brain said it, only his heart reminded him of a lifeless Gran and a Gran -5 standing behind him.

Another crack of thunder shook the earth he stood on. *FINE!* he thought defiantly. *So what if there IS such a thing as time travel?*

Test the hypothesis.

If there was a tree it was meant for Faith, not him. She was the one. His family had never moved past her death. Now, he was sure it was far more than that. So many times, he'd felt their disappointment when they looked at him. It was obvious now. They were thinking what a shame it was that the one with the talent had died.

He walked deeper into the woods and deeper into dark thoughts.

The buzzing grew louder. Except this was different. The hairs on his arms began to rise and he felt a tingling in his scalp.

Oh no—

The next lightning bolt hit like cannon fire. The ground shook beneath Finn's feet and the white light of the explosion momentarily blinded him. He fell to his knees, covering his ears. When his dimmed eyesight returned he frantically patted his arms and legs, making sure they were still intact.

"I'm okay," he said to no one but himself. Only he couldn't hear it. He couldn't hear anything except a loud ringing in his ears. He held up one hand to his ear, then checked it for blood. Nothing. He took a deep breath of relief and surveyed the damage. The scent of burnt wood and ozone was all around him, and twenty feet deeper in the woods, he saw a glow. It was a huge old oak with a seam of fire burning within it. It had taken the direct hit. The tree was lit from the inside with a molten red that gave off heat like a furnace. It was beautiful and strange.

His brain said, *A common sight after a direct lightning strike.* His heart said, *A sign.* It wasn't on the mountain and it wasn't Mom's tree, but it was enough to convince him.

He had to find Mom. Even if it meant climbing the peak and somehow finding one particular tree. He turned toward where the mountain should be, but the storm clouds hid it entirely.

He willed his legs to run, and they miraculously obeyed. He came through the trees and his feet hit the open road. There were no cars. The rain was coming at him sideways. He kept on running down the empty street, hearing the sound of his sneakers slapping against the pavement like it was happening far away.

He could make out the side of Gabi's house peeking around the back of Dorset Peak's slope. It stood there like a refuge, small and safe. Halfway up the yard, he realized he had no idea what he would say to Mrs. Rand. Gabi's mom was sure to be home this early in the morning. He couldn't say Gran was . . . dead. *Was* she? He wasn't even sure himself. He had seen her. Dead meant gone forever for most people, but she had been there talking to him, promising to see him again soon. He wasn't sure what to believe. Besides, he wasn't supposed to have been there. He wasn't supposed to know.

He changed course, heading to the back of the house. Gabi's bedroom window glowed with a warm amber light. She was awake! He rushed up to her window and banged on the glass.

Gabi nearly jumped out of her skin when she saw him standing there. He probably looked menacing, backlit by flashes of lightning. He put his hand up in a feeble attempt to reassure her that it was only him. She opened the window and he clumsily crawled in.

"Finn! What on earth are you doing?" She was both whispering and shouting at the same time.

What was he doing there? He needed to trust someone and it was Gabi. "I need help."

She put one finger to her lips and dashed out of the room, only to return a moment later with a large towel. Finn took off his sodden backpack. She draped the towel around his shoulders.

"What happened?"

All his words came out at once, like a stream of bees from a hive.

Gabi's brown eyes grew steadily wider as he spoke, and once he was finished they began to narrow in concentration.

He braced himself for the inevitable disbelief. He waited for her to jump up and yell for her mom and say he'd lost his mind. Monday at school, she'd tell all her new friends that Finn was delusional. Sebastian and his crew would laugh.

But she said, "It all makes perfect sense."

"What?!"

"Please don't take this the wrong way, Finn. Your family has always been, well, really *weird*."

I've never gotten used to traveling in and out of bad weather. You'd think by now it would be second nature. It's only gotten worse with age. It's murder on the joints.

And now, another mountain to climb. The same mountain, really. Look at it up there, taunting me. I've come to know it well. I won't be hiking the whole thing the old-fashioned way of course. That would be too difficult at my age.

I just hope this time I'll steer clear of trouble. I need to stay hidden. I don't know how many more times this body can go through that kind of punishment. My enemy has no compunctions about inflicting torture on the elderly.

It's probably because of who I am. All that rage, saved just for me.

Second thunder clap . . . fourth lightning flash . . . cue the gust of wind from the west. It's all the ticking of an enormous clock. Who would have thought I'd ever be the one saying this?

But I'm running out of time.

CHAPTER 8

The landline phone rang and they both froze. Finn heard Mrs. Rand give a cautious hello and then her voice changed, becoming serious and questioning.

"No. He's not here. What's wrong? Oh no." There was a pause and then, "Oh, I'm so sorry. No, I'll ask Gabi. I'll call back if I hear anything."

Then came the footsteps on the stairs. Panicked, Finn started for the closet. Gabi shook her head, motioning him to stay put. The door opened, and Mrs. Rand's face changed as she realized there was a sopping wet Finn standing in her daughter's room. His cheeks grew hot, even though the rest of him was still chilled to the bone.

"Hi Mom!" chirped Gabi. She somehow managed to beam a smile as if the world was completely normal. "Don't get mad. Finn is surprising his gran with her favorite muffins from the Inn before heading over. He got caught in the storm and was going to keep on going, but I forced him to come inside and wait till it passed."

Gabi was the coolest liar in the whole world. He wasn't sure if he should be impressed or afraid.

"Through the window?!" Mrs. Rand turned from Gabi to Finn, and the look on her face transformed from annoyance to sudden sympathy. "You—haven't been to your gran's yet, then?"

"No." Finn hated lying. He was sure a giant red flashing sign appeared on his forehead whenever he tried. Yet, Mrs. Rand didn't seem at all suspicious. Instead she looked positively miserable. She was steeling herself for what she had to do. She had the horrific job of telling him about Gran. He felt awful for her. He wanted to tell her he already knew, but Gabi was staring at him, silently willing him to be quiet.

He desperately tried to think what his reaction should be. He didn't know the proper response to hearing Gran had died, especially when he knew he was still going to see her again. At least she had promised that, hadn't she?

She'd also said he could trust Doc Lovell and

then her note said the exact opposite. His shoulders gave an involuntary shudder under three layers of rain-soaked clothing.

"That was your great-aunt Billie on the phone. Dr. Lovell is at your gran's now." Finn watched Mrs. Rand's neck quiver as she swallowed hard. She put her hand on his arm. "It isn't good. I'm afraid your gran passed away in her sleep."

Somehow, he felt as if he *was* hearing it for the first time it. Mrs. Rand saying those words made the whole thing real. In his world, Gran no longer existed. For the third time in his life, he had lost someone irreplaceable.

"I'm so sorry, Finn. She's gone."

He had an impossible memory of a state police officer saying those exact words—*she's gone*—to his crying parents. There was no way he could remember that.

He remembered Dad saying those same words weeks ago when Finn screamed at him to go get Mom. Dad had been slumped in his office hair, face buried in his hands. He spoke through his fingers: "I can't. She's gone."

He didn't want to hear those words ever again. Still, they echoed inside of him. He tried to speak to Mrs. Rand, to Gabi. They were looking at him, waiting. He couldn't say anything. He was falling deep inside himself. He no longer felt wet and cold. He was hollow, full of echoes. Falling, with nothing to grab on to.

She's gone.

The tears didn't come. The heart-thumping panic didn't come. There was nothing but a sense of the world being wrapped in cotton, wound over and over again. Gabi asked something and Mrs. Rand responded quietly, but he couldn't discern what their words meant. They weren't words anymore, more muffled echoes. Everything was submerged and silent as he kept falling down and down.

He landed deep inside and stayed.

ooo

Over the next few hours a few things registered in his brain. Many voices. Some of the words would stay with him.

"She'd been gone for hours . . . in her sleep . . . a mercy."

"Look at the poor boy, someone needs to reach James!"

"James is terrible about checking his messages when he's deep in research. Always drove Liz nuts."

"He can stay with us, Mom. Please."

"I need to speak to the boy." A man's angry voice. Mrs. Rand whispered back harsh words. It sounded like she pushed the visitor out to the porch, shutting the door behind her.

Finn could hear him again. It was Doc Lovell. A dark fear quietly bloomed in Finn's chest like a drop of black ink in water. Something about trust. He refused to let it wake him. He let the ink slowly dissipate and went back into his muffled world.

For the rest of the night, words and actions were performed around him. He was an uninhabited heavy planet, too full of gravity. People orbited him slowly, like cautious satellites.

Mrs. Rand gently forced him to eat something, and he took a few bites of what could have been cardboard for all he knew. This new world had no edges, no clear sounds, no taste.

At one point he found himself sitting in Gabi's kitchen staring out the window at the birds going about their business, hopping through the wet grass and chirping as if the day were like any other. He was angry at the nerve of them. And the sun, too. There shouldn't be any weather. There should be nothing at all.

She's gone. She's gone. She's gone.

(Gone)x3. The Firth equation.

He imagined writing it on an old-fashioned green chalkboard. He saw himself small and meaningless, falling away from the green like a tiny remainder, exploding in chalk dust as he hit the floor.

The echoes died away and Finn heard something different. He opened his eyes and he was home—his living room, his couch.

Gabi's hand was on his.

"Finn? Can I get you anything?" She squeezed his hand. He could feel that, a soft edge—suddenly his skin had a boundary. "We're going to stay with you, Mom and I. That's okay, right?"

There were sounds coming from across the living room, in the kitchen, nearly forgotten sounds that the house would make when someone was cooking. He looked up to see Mrs. Rand at the sink. How he wished it were Mom or Gran.

Just give me one of them back, he silently pleaded.

Gabi's arms were around his neck.

He cried into her shoulder, burying his face so she wouldn't see what he looked like raw.

CHAPTER 9

They sat in silence, eating the meal Mrs. Rand had prepared. A loud knock at the door made them all jump. Mrs. Rand got up quietly and looked out the side window.

She straightened up, took a deep breath, and went to open the door. Finn heard her reluctantly welcome Doc Lovell into a house she didn't own. From her tone, Finn got the feeling that if they were still at the Rands' cottage, where she had full authority, the door would have remained shut.

"Finn?" Mrs. Rand poked her head back into the kitchen. "Are you up to speaking to Dr. Lovell?"

Finn didn't feel up to speaking to anyone. But it was going to happen eventually—there wasn't any point in delaying it. He got up slowly and walked to the living room.

"Finn, I'm so sorry for your loss. I—I—well, you already know how much I cared for your grandmother." Doc's eyes were tinged with red, and he looked like he hadn't slept or brushed his hair in days. His second floor finally matched his first.

Looking at him, Finn began to question his own suspicions and Gran's written warning. Why shouldn't he trust Doc? He and Gran had been inseparable the last few years. Gran was happy, always laughing and acting like a teenager around him. He was nice enough to Finn, too. Still, Gran had left the note for a reason. And there was something new in Doc's tone, in the way he looked at Finn: he wanted something. Something he was sure Finn wouldn't give up easily. The problem was, Finn had no idea what that could be.

Finn put his hand into his pocket and felt Gran's note. It was real. It was his tangible proof that he didn't dream the whole thing.

"I'm trying to get ahold of your dad," Doc went on. "I've left a message on his cell and at his office at the university. I'm sure he'll call soon."

Finn nodded. He knew Mrs. Rand had been doing the same. Dad often forgot to check his phone when he was working, but he should have called back by now, he should have *been* back by now. He wasn't supposed to return till Monday night, but if he had gotten the first message he would have jumped in his car and driven home immediately.

"Finn, it looks as if your grandmother passed in her sleep from a stroke. We'll know more of course after the—by next week."

Finn heard a rustle behind him in the kitchen, and he knew both Gabi and Mrs. Rand were straining to hear.

"Have you talked to her this week, Finn? Had she spoken to you about anything . . . strange?"

"Strange?"

"Well, with a stroke there can be early warning signs—confusion, changes in behavior, even . . . delusions." The last word hung there between them like a worm on a hook.

He knew.

Finn saw it in Doc's eyes. The suspicion, the eagerness, and yes, the smoldering bead of anger under it all. Doc Lovell was angry with him, for what he still didn't know. Had he seen Finn run away from the house? Did he know what Gran had told him?

Whatever it was, Finn knew not to take the bait. "I haven't seen Gran since Wednesday night. She wasn't sick at all then." He was a little surprised at how steady his voice sounded.

Doc's eyes narrowed.

"You would know," Finn added. "You saw her that same night. Didn't you come over after I left?" Maybe that would unsettle him. Gran and Doc always went to great pains to hide whenever Doc was sleeping over.

Doc folded his arms defensively. "There was an emergency in Rupert. I didn't go over this week. I thought you were supposed to spend this whole weekend with her, Finn." It was less a question than an accusation.

"Yeah, I was heading over there when Aunt Billie called Mrs. Rand." Finn wondered if he had left behind any telltale signs that he had stayed over at Gran's last night. Had he made the bed? He couldn't remember.

So many lies bouncing around the room. If lies drifted visible like smoke, he wouldn't be able to see through the haze. Doc was staring at him, calculating. Still, Finn held his ground.

He began to think lying was something he could do well after all.

Mrs. Rand strode into the room, drying her hands

on a dishtowel. She positioned herself between the two of them, slinging the towel over her shoulder. It was a declaration of battle. She was at least a foot shorter than Doc, but she seemed to be eye-to-eye with him when she threw her shoulders back like that. Even Gabi kept her distance. She stayed in the kitchen, peeking around the doorframe.

"I should think you have all you need," said Mrs. Rand. "Unless you have something useful to report on getting ahold of James?"

"I do not. I've left a message with the library—"

"That's interesting, because I called the library as well."

Doc eyed her cautiously. "I don't see why. I told everyone, including you, that I would handle it."

"Well, I wondered if it might slip your mind. You are grieving, after all."

Doc's face was turning all shades of red and purple. Finn had the distinct impression that Mrs. Rand knew a lot more about Doc than Doc wanted her to.

"The thing is, Widener said there wasn't any appointment for a James Firth. He had not reserved a block of research time. Wouldn't they have told you the same thing?"

"Wait! Dad never got to the library? He never had an appointment?"

Mrs. Rand looked surprised to see Finn still standing there.

Doc took advantage of her distraction. "It's kind of you to help out." He picked up his coat and draped it over his arm. "Though I'm sure you realize that Finn should be with family during a time like this. If James isn't back by tomorrow, I've arranged for Finn to stay with James's cousins in Albany."

"Albany?! No!" Finn stepped forward to protest but Mrs. Rand motioned him back with a gentle touch on his arm.

"If you somehow have a reason to object to my care, Doctor, I'm sure one of his great-aunts would be happy to stay with him here. I don't think—"

"I'm sure you *don't*. Beth's sisters have health problems of their own. We know what's proper here in Vermont." Doc smiled slightly at Mrs. Rand. Finn registered the dig: Mrs. Rand was still an outsider, a flatlander. Mrs. Rand's mouth was a tight line of suppressed rage.

"Well, I won't take up any more of your time right now." With that he swiftly turned and walked out the door. He looked over his shoulder with a grim sort of smile and delivered one more parting shot: "If you do hear anything from James, you'll let me know, of course."

As soon as Doc was gone, Finn yelled, "I'm not going to Albany! I don't even know my cousins in Albany!"

"He can't possibly make Finn go! Can he?" Gabi had given up her refuge in the kitchen and was looking as pained as Finn.

Mrs. Rand's look of anger dissipated and was replaced with one of defeat. "I don't know what he's capable of doing. Technically, I don't have any rights to care for you, Finn. We need to get ahold of your father. Can you think of anywhere else he might be?"

He could be researching somewhere else. He could be looking for Mom.

He could have just left.

No, he wouldn't. Not even this new Dad would do that to him.

"Maybe it was another library and you heard wrong? Is there a list we can try?"

"There are two or three he's been to a lot. I'm absolutely positive he said it was Widener." As much as they'd clashed lately, Finn wanted Dad back now. Dad wouldn't let Doc send him off to Albany.

"Dr. Lovell was content with making everyone think a message was on its way to your dad, when it obviously wasn't. For some reason, he doesn't want your dad here." Mrs. Rand paused and made sure Finn was holding her gaze. "Can you think of any reason why?"

Gabi gave him a nearly imperceptible shake of her head. *Don't trust anyone.* He had no idea if that was supposed to include Mrs. Rand. It seemed wrong to distrust her when she was so obviously concerned for him.

"I can't," he said.

Mrs. Rand gave him a resigned nod and headed back into the kitchen. He'd been wrong about the lying. It was still hard. It all depended on who you were lying to.

CHAPTER 10

"We can't tell your mom. She'd never let me hike up that mountain," Finn said.

Gabi didn't look happy; maybe lying wasn't as easy for her either. Mrs. Rand was on the phone in the kitchen, dialing down the list Finn had given her of Dad's usual research haunts. Gabi and Finn were planted on the giant sectional sofa. She nestled in the crook with her tablet and he sat against the farthest armrest with his knees up to his chest.

"Don't you mean she'd never let *us* hike it?" Gabi demanded.

Oh, so that was why she was frowning. "Gabi, I think I should go by myself. You can cover for me." It made sense. If Doc came looking for him, she could throw him off track, at least for a little while.

"What?! No!" Gabi stood up, letting the tablet

fall to the carpet.

"I've got to go before Doc ships me off to Albany. It's got to be tomorrow."

"There is absolutely no way you get to do this without me," she said, her hands defiantly on her hips.

Finn bit back the urge to snap that this wasn't a game. He had an entire mountain to search for one single tree. It could take days.

"Listen, I don't know why he wants me out of town so fast. All I know is Gran said not to trust anyone—"

"So you're not going to trust me?"

"That's not what I meant."

Gabi's arms dropped to her sides. "Then I'm going with you. Settled."

"I don't want you in danger."

"From who? Doc?" Her eyes went wide.

"No—I don't know." Finn wondered if he was being paranoid. How could Doc suddenly be his enemy? It was obvious he loved Gran. And yet . . . "I mean, I do think he's hiding something."

"Yeah, like he didn't actually call your dad."

"Exactly!"

"That *was* weird." Gabi picked up the tablet, placed it back on the sofa and sat down again with a confused look on her face.

"Your mom doesn't like him," Finn remarked. "Why?"

Gabi shifted slightly and didn't look Finn in the eye. "Come on, Finn. He's one of *those* locals. Referred to Mom as 'that city gal' for two years after we moved in. Mom suspects he's why she's never been invited to join any of the town boards. He hasn't given her any reason to like him."

"Yeah," said Finn. "It does take him a long time to accept flatlanders."

Gabi stared at him open-mouthed for a second before she asked, "Well, how long does it take him to accept Puerto Ricans? Because I think that's his real problem."

Now it was Finn's turn to stare. "Whoa. You think Doc is racist?"

"He sure wasn't very welcoming to my mom."

Finn had never considered this possiblity. "I just thought he disliked every flatlander."

"That's possible, I suppose. Forget it."

Finn doubted he would, nor did he think Gabi could. He trusted Doc even less now.

"There's a bit more to why Mom dislikes him so much, though," Gabi went on. "She told me not to say anything because we couldn't be sure. Only Mom certainly *seems* sure, the way she talked to him this morning."

Finn was even more shocked. "Gabi, I've told you every secret I've ever had!"

"I'm sorry! It wasn't my secret to tell." She had pulled a loose thread from the sofa cushion and was winding it around her forefinger. She let it go and it unraveled and fell back onto the tablet's sleeping screen, a blue squiggle on black ice.

"Talk."

"I saw Doc and your great-aunt Billie together last month in Manchester, when Mom and I stopped by the café across from Northshire. They were arguing in whispers. It looked like the kind of argument you have with a girlfriend, not your girlfriend's sister." Gabi scrunched up her nose. "You know, we still need a better term for that."

Finn felt the anger rise inside of him. Could Doc have cheated on Gran with her own sister? "Are you sure?"

"I mean, maybe it was nothing," she said. "It felt weird to me, that's all. Mom said she's also seen them together a lot when she travels to Rupert for theater supplies. Mom thought it was super creepy of him, but she had no proof. She said she wouldn't put it past your great-aunt Billie either. Everyone in town says she was always jealous of your gran."

It was infuriating that everyone knew more about his family than he did. "Yeah, she's always been that way. Gran told me Aunt Billie was in love with my Grandpa Jack, way back when they were young. But this . . ."

"Maybe she still wants whatever her sister has."

Finn remembered the notebooks Aunt Billie obsessively kept and wondered if it was possible that she was still the same jealous girl.

"Did they see you?"

"I'm very good at not being seen when I don't want to be." Gabi picked up the blue thread again and this time wound it around her pinkie. She looked embarrassed. "Listen, it's not like I told this story to anyone else. I just told my mom, and she's not part of the Dorset gossip machine. You know that."

"It's just I thought I knew all the gossip about us. I guess I didn't."

"Ugh. Why would you want to? It's better not to listen."

He wasn't so sure about that. If he'd known all the rumors, he might've at least asked the right questions. "It doesn't make sense, though. Why would Doc be interested in Aunt Billie? She's nothing at all like Gran."

"Who knows? Maybe he just liked the extra attention."

"Well, I think Doc is hiding something more than just Aunt Billie." He went back to his prime objective. "And I think you need to stay behind when I go to the mountain. There's no way of knowing what will happen. And if I'm not back by a certain time, you can send help."

Gabi leaned toward him, her eyes locked on his. "Don't you dare try to do this without me. You need me along. You don't know the first thing about hiking."

She was right, of course. He never hiked. It was his parents' thing. He wasn't exactly an outdoorsy kind of guy, but he wasn't going to let that stand in his way now.

"How hard can it be? You follow a trail up and then you come back down."

That was the wrong thing to say. Gabi geared up for one of her lectures. "It's easy to get lost on those trails. I know what to do. I've been up the Equinox a couple of times with Mr. Schuman's outdoors club.

I even have telescoping poles." She had her arms folded in front of her, her face daring him to ask what telescoping poles were. He had no idea and she knew it. She offered the answer without prompting.

"They're like professional metal walking sticks. Mom won them at the Founder's Day picnic. They come in real handy on steep climbs. See? You need me. You know nothing."

"I know that a broken branch can probably do the same thing and that three hikes with Mr. Schuman does not make you an expert."

"Stop arguing. We need to find a trail map."

Hiking with a partner did make more sense. And he had to admit, if only to himself, he'd feel better if she was with him. It was a selfish want. He wasn't proud of it.

They spent the next twenty minutes online looking for maps or trail guides.

"Dorset Peak must be a boring hike. All I'm finding are a few peakbagger blogs saying it's nothing special," Finn said.

"What's a peakbagger?"

"Oh, so now I get to teach you something about hiking!" He raised an eyebrow at her, but thought better of it when he saw her face. When Gabi got annoyed she was like a puffed-up little sparrow. It was fun to watch her hop around angrily at first, but he'd pay for it later. There was no time for that.

"They're hikers who want to bag every peak. They're not in it for the hike itself or the view, they just have a checklist of mountains they want to conquer."

"You just learned that online, didn't you?"

"Yes," he admitted, smiling for the first time in ages.

She scooted up closer to him and looked at his screen. "Any maps? Hints about the trail?" she asked.

"Nothing. Can't we just get on the trail and continue in the direction of up?"

"That's the fastest way to get lost. Those trails always overlap."

Finn continued to click and scroll, desperately looking for something resembling a map. If they didn't have to be so secretive they could just walk over to the Inn and grab one from the front desk, but they couldn't risk someone noticing them. Then it hit him: they were making this more difficult than it needed to be.

"Hang on! My Dad probably has a guide book in his office!"

That burst of confidence dissipated when he opened the door and saw the state of his father's usually pristine workplace. It looked like someone had ransacked it, only he knew that someone was Dad. He had been sloppier lately, but Finn had no idea it had gotten this bad.

"How can he find anything in here?" Gabi stepped gingerly over stacks of books, trying not to topple them onto the carpet. At least, Finn *thought* he remembered a carpet. He pushed some paper aside with his toes. Yep, the maroon oriental rug was still there.

"It's always been so neat I was afraid to come in here. Things must be a lot worse than I thought."

Finn waded over to the desk, where printouts of newspaper articles from the 1800s were at least four inches deep across the whole surface. This was typical; that was Dad's favorite century, and he loved having physical copies of research materials.

Finn turned around to scan the shelves. Their contents weren't new to him. Mostly old books, a few paperweights and academic awards, a snow globe, and the framed photograph of the quarry. Why his father would keep a picture of that horrible place was beyond him. But now, as he studied it up close, he realized that there were two tiny far-off people in the quarry picture. He never noticed them before. Two small children, sitting on one of the marble slabs with their backs to the camera. A boy and a girl.

Finn picked up the photo and studied it carefully. It was Faith that gave them away. Her massive head of red hair was unmistakable. Her curls were catching the sun and Finn could almost touch the memory of them. He wondered if this was the last picture taken of them together. How could he have never noticed they were in it before? His eyes drifted to the small orange digital numbers on the bottom right. A timestamp made by the camera, dated more than a year after Faith's death. Dad probably couldn't bear to develop the film until then.

"What's that?" Gabi asked from her lookout point near the doorway.

"Just a picture my dad took." Finn placed the frame back on the shelf and with it, the memory. It would hold till later.

He found what he was looking for on the bottom dust-covered shelf: a trail guide for southern Vermont. "This should have what we need." He held it up for Gabi to see.

"My mom's coming! Hide it!"

Mrs. Rand entered and looked around. "I hope your father is more organized in his head than he is in here!"

Finn forced a chuckle. The thick paperback was painfully wedged between his waistband and lower back.

"What are you two looking for?" Mrs. Rand asked.

"Finn thought we might find information about another library his dad might have gone to."

Mrs. Rand looked instantly hopeful. "Any luck?"

"No," Finn replied. It wasn't truly a lie.

"Well then," Mrs. Rand sighed, "I'm afraid we just have to trust he'll be home when he said he would. I'm sure he'll be here tomorrow night. Meanwhile, I'm going into town to talk to Mr. Abernathy. Maybe he can help me find a legal way to delay Dr. Lovell."

She was doing her best to sound positive but her voice was full of defeat.

ooo

Finn and Gabi made a plan. They'd meet in the hallway at four a.m., leave through the French doors in

Dad's office, walk to Gabi's house, get the equipment they needed, and pack some food and water from her fridge. Then they would walk in the dark to the main trailhead next to Gran's house, where they'd wait for the sun to come up. As soon as it was light enough, they could begin the climb.

"What about my mom?" Gabi asked as they sat in Finn's room. "She'll freak out when she realizes we're missing. And reception is terrible on the mountain, so we won't even be able to text her once we're up there."

There was a long silence. They had never been risk takers. Well, maybe Gabi took a few more than he did, but they both tended to be cautious. It was what remainders did. He stole a sidewise glance at her. She was a remainder, too.

Finn and Gabi never spoke about what they had in common, but they both knew how important it was to stay safe. You live an extra careful life, never wanting to make your parents relive the pain. Remainders aren't whole numbers, but they are better than negatives. You could never become a negative. Another negative would destroy the whole equation.

Gabi shifted her gaze over Finn's head, looking skeptically at the Periodic Table of Elements he had tacked to the wall. He wondered for a moment if she was also thinking about them in terms of unstable equations. No, of course not. It was his weird Finn way of understanding it. Gabi wasn't about science. Her explanations were always something mystical, something not grounded in reality at all. Something he wished he could believe in as much as she did. Maybe now he could. Why not? He believed in time travel now. Who knew what he'd believe in tomorrow.

"I'm sure your mom won't be *that* worried," Finn said, though the words rang hollow. He tried not to imagine Dad coming home early after all and finding Finn gone. He didn't want to think about Dad being all alone. The last few weeks had changed him enough.

"You aren't supposed to hike without telling someone," she countered. "What if—something happens—and we need help and no one knows where we've gone?"

"Good point," Finn said. Then he had an idea. "We could time an email to be delivered later. We could set it up tonight and have it send tomorrow around dinnertime. We should be back by then, but if we're not the email will explain where we've gone."

Gabi nodded, looking reassured. "Yeah, we should be covered that way. If we do get in trouble on the mountain, someone will know where we are."

"Right," Finn agreed with false confidence. Inside his head a small doubting voice added, *Even if it might be too late.*

CHAPTER 11

The rest of the evening passed with Mrs. Rand hovering over them, offering a neverending supply of snacks. Everything still tasted like wet newspaper to Finn, but he nibbled at whatever she gave him anyway. He didn't want to disappoint her, and the guilt over what they were about to put her through rested heavy on his conscience. Come tomorrow afternoon, she was going to be sick with worry and it would be all his fault.

She had the Inn deliver dinner. They sat around making small talk, with Mrs. Rand watching him carefully. Finn felt like he was between specimen glass on a microscope. He wanted to assure her he wasn't going to disappear inside himself again, though he couldn't be sure if that was true. Whenever he remembered Gran lying there, lifeless, it made him want to go back and hide. But he only needed to look out the nearest window to snap himself out of it. The peak was there, waiting for him.

Alone in his room that night, he knew he should be sleeping, but instead he was staring at the familiar web of shadows the tree branches made on his ceiling. He always slept with the blinds open. He liked the moon shadows and he preferred to be woken by daylight.

An entire mountain covered in thousands of trees, and he was going to find one specific one. His mother must have made it clear somehow. He had to trust her.

He gave up the pretense of sleep and rolled over, reaching under the mattress where he had stowed the trail guide. There was enough moonlight to read by—his favorite kind of night. Based on the map and the trail description, the hike didn't sound too difficult. There were a few places where the trail split, but the guide said it was all well marked.

His eyelids began to feel heavy. In only a few hours his phone alarm would wake him, long before the sun would. The moonlit branches trembled in the wind, occasionally pawing against his window with a light scratching noise. These were soothing sounds to Finn, sounds of home.

It was the sudden quick pounding that was different. Like a large bird hitting the window—or the muffled smack of a hand against the window pane.

He sat up in bed and stared at his window, waiting for it to happen again. Then he saw the shadow. It was hunched over, a bulky human form that went by too quickly, in an unnatural kind of stutter-step.

Finn jumped out of bed and pushed his back up to the far wall in terror.

Thud. Then the shadow. Then gone.

Finn approached the window cautiously and mustered up enough courage to look outside.

On the slate patio, a good twenty feet away, someone was pacing back and forth. The movement was all wrong though. It wasn't a normal walk; it was a disconcerting lurch, the way something in a horror movie moves when it's only pretending to be human.

The figure stopped. Its head turned slowly, directly toward the window.

Finn jumped backward on pure instinct and fell over his desk chair with a thud. Sprawled on his bedroom carpet, he looked up at the window and realized the face staring at him was slowly resolving into a known entity.

Aunt Ev motioned for him to open the window.

He instinctively obeyed, hurrying to his feet and throwing up the sash.

"It took you long enough! Get dressed. We have work to do!"

She was wearing layers and layers of coats and what looked like at least five pairs of gloves. It made her look like a giant boulder on feet.

"Well? Do as I say, boy! I know you've learned how to respect your elders. Get out here before someone sees me!"

He pulled on the same pair of jeans he'd been wearing for the last few days and felt the crinkle of Gran's note in his pocket. He considered leaving it behind, but thought it would be safer with him than left in the room. He couldn't afford to lose it. It was still the only proof he had.

Aunt Ev was waiting for him in the shadows beyond the patio. "Come on. We don't have a lot of time." With that, she began striding into the woods.

"Where are we going?" Finn demanded, eyes wide.

"You're going to have to trust me. We'll be right back. I promise."

Finn looked back at the house. "I need to get Gabi."

"What?"

"I'm not going anywhere without Gabi."

"Really?" She didn't sound angry, just confused. She muttered something under her breath that sounded like "This is new." Finn couldn't be sure. After a moment she nodded. "Fine. Hurry up about it! Don't go through the house. Go to the window."

ooo

"Where is she taking us?" Gabi was still rubbing her eyes as she pulled the chair closer to the window.

"I don't know." Finn held his hand out to steady her.

"And you trust her?"

"Yeah, I mean no. I guess I don't know, but I want to know more about my family's secrets and this might be one way to find out."

The look on Gabi's face was a mixture of annoyance and resignation. "You realize we're supposed to climb a whole mountain in five hours? Sleep is usually a good idea beforehand."

"I don't know about you, but I wasn't sleeping. And we can't start the hike until sunup. Do you want to stay here?"

"I'm coming." She continued her climb down to the patio. "But if my mother finds out I'll be grounded till I'm thirty."

They padded across the slate as silently as they could, past the window of the guest room Gabi's mother was sleeping in.

Aunt Ev was flapping her arms in agitation. "Hurry! No talking now, follow me."

"Not till you tell us where we're going." Finn wasn't about to lose control of the situation.

"Oh for the love of Pete! You're determined to make this difficult for me, aren't you? Don't be coy, boy! I know you know. There's no way my sister, accomplished Future Traveler that she was, would leave this mortal coil without saying good-bye to her one and only grandson."

Finn folded his arms, refusing to confirm her hypothesis. "Where. Are. We. Going?"

"To a very important meeting. One you should've been to a long time ago." She was angry and defiant, like she was righting a longstanding wrong.

"Who meets at one o'clock in the morning?" Gabi asked.

She glared at Gabi. "You've never been here before, little bird girl. You sure you want a part of this?"

Gabi's shoulders stiffened. Finn recognized that stance. Gabi was pulling herself up to her full height, which wasn't much at all. If you knew her, you knew what was coming next, a speech that would likely make you think twice about calling her "little" ever again. Finn stepped between them.

"Yes, she wants a part of this." He turned back to Gabi. "You do, right?"

Gabi peered out from behind Finn and looked Aunt Ev in the eye. "Tell the old lady I'm in."

"You still didn't answer her question. Who meets at one in the morning?"

"Iztah. That's who."

"Iztah?" He said it hesitantly, testing the name on his tongue. He'd never heard it before in his life.

"I-S-T-A. The International Society for Temporal Adherence, currently devoid of competent leadership, thanks to my fool sister!"

Finn looked at Gabi, half expecting her to say she'd heard of it. She shook her head.

"If you two are done wasting my valuable seconds, will you please follow me?"

Aunt Ev walked impossibly fast for a woman in her sixties, or was it her seventies? Finn wasn't exactly sure how old she was, only that she was Gran's youngest sister. She was leading them through the woods and out toward town. The moonlight gave the forest trail enough light for him to see where her feet landed. Finn made sure to follow closely, and Gabi was directly behind him.

"Why International?" he asked Aunt Ev.

"Oh, I insisted on it when I moved to Italy for a few years in the seventies. Beth added it mostly to placate me."

He ran over their conversation in his mind as they walked. "Why did you call Gran a Future Traveler?"

"Most of us can only go backward and return. Billie, bless her heart, can't even manage that anymore, except by accident. But your gran and your mother could go *forward* in time. Though each time they did it, it took its toll." Her lips trembled and her face contorted in sadness for a second before she regained composure with an impatient shake of her head.

She made a sharp turn, and Finn caught the stutter-step of her movements again. She seemed to be rebuffering in reality. It was the oddest thing to watch. He turned to catch Gabi's face and he could tell that she was seeing it, too.

"Aunt Ev, how come you're moving like that? Like an old filmstrip missing frames?"

Gabi scowled at him for giving up their new secret. The truth was Finn felt safe in revealing it because Gabi had witnessed it as well.

"Ahhh." Aunt Ev smiled over her shoulder. "That's because I'm doubling too close to my Initial. An Initial is the version of ourselves that belongs in the time period we're in. When we Travel back, or double, in close proximity to our Initial, we can appear sort of funny. And, well, I'm an *old lady*"—she raised a mocking eyebrow at Gabi—"not as good at this as I once was."

Gabi looked away, and Finn thought if it wasn't so dark out he'd see her blush.

Aunt Ev nodded at Finn. "Good observation. If I'm right about you, Finn, you'll start noticing a whole lot more soon enough."

He felt a leap of something akin to hope, only to be replaced with the familiar sinking in the pit of his stomach. "There's nothing special about me. Gran said boys don't Travel."

"But there might be other things you can offer. We don't really know about you yet, Finn. Do we? That's what this meeting is about. Hurry up, now. It's already started. We'll sneak in and hide in the choir loft."

The choir loft? They were going to the church? Apparently his family's secret time-traveling society was meeting like an after-school youth group.

"What happens if someone sees us?" Gabi asked.

"Well, you're not supposed to be there. Doc and his cronies don't want Finn finding out about our Traveling for several more years." She glanced back at them over a long nubby gray scarf that was wrapped many times around her neck. "If they see you, they'll know I've broken the rules. If they see *you*"—she pointed a fat gloved finger at Gabi—"well, you don't want to know."

Don't trust anyone. The words were still in Finn's pocket.

"Why is Doc involved? He's not part of our family." The more Finn thought about Doc, the more it felt like he had no reason to be *anywhere.*

"ISTA is more than our family. This town has been keeping our secret for generations. There's a trusted circle of those closest to us."

If Aunt Ev trusted Doc, then Finn would have to watch her closely. He certainly couldn't share Gran's note with her now.

"Won't they notice you missing?" Finn asked as he struggled to keep pace with her.

For the first time, Aunt Ev looked genuinely amused. "I'm already there, m'boy. You really haven't got the hang of this yet, have you?"

"No," he said. "I definitely haven't."

CHAPTER 12

They stayed close to the backyards and sparse strips of woods that stood between the small houses. All the houses in the center of town were painted the same, white with green shutters. In the moonlight they faded to gray and black. It wasn't often that Finn saw Dorset in the middle of the night, and for the first time he was struck by the beauty of the pale marble sidewalks crisscrossing the green, which would now be more aptly named "the black" in the moonlight. The grass appeared all the darker surrounded by the bright shimmer of the marble, stretching before him like a lunar mirror.

"It's beautiful, isn't it?" said Aunt Ev, watching him closely.

"I never noticed how the marble looks at night. It glows."

"Every inch of it is Dorset marble, that is. That whole mountain is filled with it," Aunt Ev said proudly.

"We learned about it in school," Gabi said.

"You learned nothing, girl!" Aunt Ev's temper flashed again. "They told you what? How the business of gutting that mountain created our town? You learned about economics. You learned about rock. It's not rock. Did you know marble has veins? That it breathes? That it's made of minerals that also live inside you? You kids, you think of that mountain like it's a big dead thing in the distance. You use that old quarry as a swimming pool, forgetting what it really is. It's more than a hole in the ground. It's a *scar*!"

Finn shuddered at the word. He didn't need to be told that. It was the biggest scar his family had.

Aunt Ev seemed to realize what she was saying and to whom. Her voice immediately softened. "Mountains have roots, you know. You can't go digging up roots and expect everything to continue on the same."

"The marble has something to do with Travelers?" Gabi's interest was piqued and no flash of temper could scare her off. Finn knew that tone of voice.

It was the same one she got when she talked about unexplained phenomena, when she was inventing the fantastic middle ground between what was known and what wasn't. Now it looked like she had found an ally in Aunt Ev. Finn felt outnumbered.

"I believe it's what allows us to Travel. Once we leave Dorset, no one in our family has been able to Travel at all. It also keeps us grounded. It's what ties us to the time we're born in." She reached into the many folds of her jackets and pulled out a small, smooth white stone. "We all carry a grounding stone with us. This is how we stay where we need to be."

"But it's just a rock!" Finn was still having a hard time accepting the absurdity of it all.

Aunt Ev rose up on him like a viper. She came up so close to him that he could see the broken red blood vessels against the whites of her eyes.

"Just a rock? If I poured a handful of sand into your palm you'd probably say it was just sand, wouldn't you?"

"Yes. Yes, I would."

"Fool! Without sand and a well-timed bolt of lightning, you wouldn't have glass. Without glass, no telescopes, no microscopes, none of your computers! You can trace each grain back to the original exploded star it came from. Everything your precious science relies on rests on a pile of sand."

Finn's instinct was to note that it was far more complicated than that, that it was really about the mineral silica. But something else was nagging at him, pulling at the back of his brain.

Aunt Ev leaned in and whispered right into his ear. "You need to start thinking bigger and further back than your silly books. Much further back."

Much. Further. Back.

He had the momentary sensation of being connected to everything and everyone. A universe inside of his brain was suddenly switched on, and then just as quickly, it was summarily shut down. It was like he was on the verge of understanding a mathematic formula only to have someone pull it away. He couldn't hold on to the thought.

Aunt Ev eyed him warily for a moment and then grew sheepish. "I'm sorry. I'm told I get a bit combative when my ideas are challenged. I find I hold on to my best ideas when I'm in a state of agitation. Makes me terrible company though. Here." Aunt Ev grabbed his hand, turned it, and placed her grounding stone firmly in his palm. It felt cold and smooth, and he curled his fingers around it instinctively. "You take it. I know you're not a Traveler, but maybe it will bring you luck."

"Don't you need it?"

"I have more. You take that one. No arguments now."

The stone began to feel warm against his skin. Almost like it had a pulse.

Finn turned to look at Dorset Peak and was surprised to not be able to make out its full outline in the night sky. He knew it was there though, like always. What Aunt Ev was saying would certainly explain why the family had stayed in Dorset for so many generations.

He thought about telling her about the tree. He knew it should stay a secret, but at the same time he needed to find out what Aunt Ev knew.

He decided to approach the topic carefully. "Is there such a thing as a time portal? Like, for people who aren't born with the ability to Travel?" Finn was surprised to hear how desperate and leading he sounded. He didn't dare look at Gabi, but he felt her watching him, worried he was about to give up the secret.

"A portal? You've seen too many movies. There is no way for non-Travelers to Travel. No time machines, no doorways in the space-time continuum.

This is a genetic gift. A skill we're born with and then hone over time." She straightened her spine, making Finn think she was about to brag about her accomplishments. The next words out of her mouth proved him wrong.

"Your mother is the best, you know. She can go whenever she wishes, without so much as a blip. She was a pro from when she was your age. Each generation gets better at it, each mother surpassed by her own daughter."

The word *daughter* hit Finn like a slap. He could see it in Aunt Ev's eyes, what he saw in everyone's eyes: Mom, Dad, Gran. The deep sorrow for what ended with Faith, and the disappointment in what was left behind.

Him.

Aunt Ev led Finn and Gabi around to the back of the local church. Pausing at the back door, she pulled back her gloves to expose a device on her wrist. It was black and shiny gold. The face was hugely clunky, with a digital window and many buttons. Maybe there was some sort of scientific equipment involved in Traveling after all! Finn leaned in eagerly and noticed it had what looked like an old calculator under the liquid crystal.

"Picked it up last week in 1982 along with a pair of fuschia leg warmers. Nicked them to be honest." She rotated her wrist to get the full view of the watch. "Handy little thing, quite accurate. The eighties weren't all fluff." She pulled her glove back over the giant watch and gave each of them a stern look. "Now come on. There's a lot you can learn here tonight. Don't make a sound, and follow me when I walk. Halt when I do. Duck when I do. Watch my every move. Be my shadow. Got it?"

They both nodded and followed her into the church.

CHAPTER 13

Aunt Ev brought them past the back offices, through an old wooden door with a pointed top. They stood in silence while Aunt Ev consulted her retro megawatch once more. She counted to twelve under her breath and then opened the heavy wooden door to the large main room. Finn rushed to follow her and was shocked to find the building brightly lit and full of noise.

The main room was packed with people arguing and trying to talk over each other. Finn, Gabi, and Aunt Ev were now in plain view—only no one was looking at them. Aunt Ev strode in like she was invisible. Not knowing what else to do, Finn and Gabi followed as closely as they could. After taking a few strides, Aunt Ev crouched behind a row of battered maroon folding chairs. Finn and Gabi did the same.

Finn heard a familiar woman's voice rise louder than the rest: "We shouldn't be doing this without Will. It can wait till he's back!" This was followed by the quick staccato of angry heel clicks coming right toward them. Finn was sure they were about to be discovered. He shot Aunt Ev a look of panic. She gave him and Gabi a placid smile.

The clicking heels belonged to Aunt Billie. She came right up to their row. The laces of her gray boots were only a foot away from Finn's own toes. He hadn't seen her in almost a year, since Gran's big Thanksgiving dinner. She and Aunt Ev had argued and it hadn't ended well, even with Gran doing her best to calm them down. He was shocked at how much frailer Aunt Billie looked. He looked away quickly so she wouldn't feel his eyes on her. All she had to do was glance down and she would see them hiding there.

Only she didn't. Her eyes remained focused on the front of the room.

"You're all fools!" she snapped. "You have no idea what you're messing with!" As the crowd continued to argue, she spun on the noisy heels and stormed out of the building. Finn turned to Aunt Evelyn to silently communicate his astonishment, but she was already crawling across the room on all fours. He and Gabi had to rush to catch up.

She stopped at the stairs to the choir loft, stood up nonchalantly, and brushed the dust off her coat and skirt. Finn's neck was practically on a swivel. He kept checking to see if anyone in the room was looking their way. Gabi's hand gripped his forearm. She was just as nervous, but the attendees were still in a heated argument. Aunt Evelyn checked her watch again and waved them up the small wooden stairs. Finn let Gabi go first, then began climbing as quietly as he could. Aunt Ev followed him closely.

Another voice he knew echoed through the church. "I am standing by this motion. I think we should bring Finn into this!"

Finn stopped short in the middle of the staircase at the sound of his name. It was Aunt Ev's voice coming from across the room. It seemed impossible, with Aunt Ev also standing right below him on the stairs, but there she was in the middle of the crowd. She was arguing with the others—about him. Only now the other version of her was also prodding him with a gloved fist to keep him climbing up the narrow staircase.

As he looked out over the pews he realized that the Aunt Ev in the meeting looked strange. She had a shimmer around her, like the haze that comes off a hot road in the heat of summer. The air around her was wavy. No one else appeared to notice. Finn wanted to ask Gabi if she saw it too, but that question would have to wait. Aunt Ev was pushing him from behind.

It was a great vantage point. There had to be at least thirty people below them. He knew every one of them, too. Mrs. Henreatty, the front desk clerk at the Inn, was in a heated side discussion with the mail carrier, Mr. Booth. Mr. Wells, the town manager, shook his head disapprovingly and Mrs. Allen, the head of the Dorset Historical Society, chimed in sternly with, "This has historically been up to the immediate family!"

"Well, the boy has no immediate family to speak for him now, does he? I say it's time we intervene." It was the shimmery Aunt Ev who responded so adamantly.

The Aunt Ev behind him on the stairs gave him a shove that nearly brought him to his knees. It also brought him to his senses, enough to duck low and keep moving. Gabi was already crouched and watching at the end of the loft. He settled in close to her. They still had to be quiet, but at least up here they were well hidden.

Aunt Ev silently closed the floor hatch over the staircase. Finn looked around for the nearest way out. Aside from the stairs, the loft had two doors on either side. He hoped they were both exits and not closets. He'd never been up to the choir loft before. The only time he even went to church was when Gran dragged him. His parents' idea of worship was a quiet hike or a picnic.

Mr. Wells spoke above the fray: "How do we know Beth hasn't taken care of this already?"

Several voices chimed in.

"We don't."

"You're right!"

"Wouldn't Finn show up here at the meeting if she had?" Mrs. Henreatty asked.

Mr. Wells said, "I say we wait till Doc returns with James. They'll decide." He folded his arms and stretched his legs out in front of him, crossing one ankle over the other as if this punctuated all arguments.

Finn's mouth twisted. Doc was only pretending to find Dad. He wondered if anyone here actually knew that.

The shimmery Aunt Ev opened her mouth as if to say something, then thought better of it. She paced back and forth, then looked up at the choir loft. Finn swore she smiled at him.

"That's when I got the idea to bring you here," the Aunt Ev next to him whispered. "I'm simply ravishing when I'm full of a good plan, aren't I?" She poked her head up and gave a small wave to herself down below. The whole thing made Finn feel rather queasy.

Shimmery Aunt Ev turned back to the group. "I think we should plan it, then. We haven't practiced an initiation in ages. We should go over the syllabus."

Finn leaned forward. This was why Aunt Ev brought him here. He was going to get all his family's secrets at once.

"What's the point, Evelyn? He can't Travel, he's a boy!" Mr. Wells was now sitting up, with his fancy boots pulled in under his chair.

"Well, it couldn't hurt!" Several people began muttering to each other.

"Doc said we should wait until he's eighteen. That was the plan, or have you forgotten?" It was Mr. Wells again.

"But that was before everything happened!" said Mrs. Wells. "He'll have to be told now. He could become a valuable asset, just like James."

"Joan . . ." He silenced his wife with only her first name. She folded her hands in her lap and lowered her head. Finn grimaced. If Mom or Gran were here, they would've been furious to see Mrs. Wells being treated like that.

"It's all so sad," sighed Ms. Alister, the woman who had cut his hair since he was a baby. "We thought we'd be doing this with Faith right around now."

Out of the corner of his eye, Finn saw Gabi's head turn his way, but he refused to meet her gaze. He pushed his fist into his stomach and pressed hard, willing the tightness to go away.

The group below was silent and thoughtful for a few seconds. Finn knew that somber pause all too well.

Shimmery Aunt Ev resumed, "I think Beth and Liz would want us to do this." There was a brief silence and Finn noted a lot of heads bobbing up and down. Even Mr. Wells was silenced by the mention of Finn's mother and grandmother.

No one else in the room noticed that Aunt Ev was radiating a weird energy. Finn couldn't tell whether it was invisible to them or if they were just used to it.

"We *will* need to welcome him soon, and we may as well practice." The shimmery Aunt Ev was once again all business.

Mr. Abernathy, Dorset's only lawyer, chimed in. "I think this is all a waste of time, but if you want to go over the syllabus, I suppose we can put it up to a vote. I move to refer the motion to committee—"

"Oh for goodness sake," said shimmery Aunt Ev, "let's not start with that Rules of Order hogwash! Those in favor, raise your hands."

"Ev, you could at least move to suspend rules!" Mr. Abernathy was obviously upset with this lack of ceremony.

"Move yourself, Tom! You may be the town's only legal light, but sometimes you're a bit dim." She kicked the leg of his chair and Mr. Abernathy flinched, then instantly looked abashed for doing so. Finn began to wonder who was in charge. That's when he remembered what Aunt Ev had said in the woods.

It was Gran. Gran had been the leader of ISTA. Only she could keep this unruly bunch in order.

"Raise your hand and say 'aye' if you think we should go over primary syllabus to prepare for Finn's initiation."

Finn counted hands carefully. The ayes had it by at least seven up-stretched arms. He was trying to memorize who was on his side when a loud noise came from the left side of the church.

The sound of a door opening and then slamming.

"I've decided to stay after all!" Aunt Billie announced. She strode proudly up to the shimmery Aunt Ev, her gray hair tied back in her ever-present tight bun, her stick thin arms crossed over each other in smug victory. Next to plump, pink-cheeked Aunt Ev, she looked like a pale ghost. Now she had that fuzzy halo around her too, waves of energy that no one else seemed to notice.

The Aunt Ev next to Finn grabbed his wrist in panic. "She's not supposed to come back!"

Aunt Billie gave the shimmery Aunt Ev a sidelong glance, then sauntered over to the choir loft, obviously enjoying the fact that all eyes in the room were on her. She looked up and her face was full of smug victory.

She knew they were up there.

"We have to go. Now." Aunt Ev pushed Finn toward Gabi, toward the small side door at the top.

He grabbed Gabi's arm as they passed her, and she stumbled after him. There was no time to make a quiet exit. Their shoes made a racket across the wooden floor of the loft.

As they made their way through the small walkway they were greeted by another Aunt Billie, leaning up against the far wall, arms folded in nonchalant triumph. This Aunt Billie was not shimmering. When she stepped forward, Finn saw her movements stutter-step like Aunt Ev's in the yard.

That's it! Finn thought. If you were in the same time and place as your Initial, you stutter-stepped, just like Aunt Ev had said. But there was more to it: while you were doubling there, your Initial also shimmered. He wanted to ask Aunt Ev if he had it right. If that was the case, why didn't everyone in the meeting realize that Aunt Ev was doubling?

"I figured you out, Evelyn." This Aunt Billie was wearing a matching hat and scarf, and a giant purple puffy coat. It made her legs look all the more skeletal. She was dressed for January, not September, and cold was still radiating off her. Her face was pale as snow, not even a red-tipped nose or flush in the cheek. The lines etched in her face seemed twice as deep as the last time he had seen her up close. "This was your dumbest idea yet. You're a misinformed meddler! He's a boy! He is not capable of helping."

Finn registered the words and waited for the feeling of emptiness, preparing himself to push it away. Only this time, he felt something else. She was wrong. Deep down inside him there was a truth that was coming to the surface. There had to be something he could do or Mom wouldn't have left him instructions.

Footsteps sounded in the hallway behind them. Finn could hear the other Aunt Billie leading them. "I know I heard something! I told you we need to consider better security." Her voice held a theatrical quality. She sounded like a bad actress in a school play—someone who knows exactly how the scene is going to end, but pretends not to.

Aunt Ev's fists were curled up inside her gloves. "Let us by, Billie," she said to Aunt Billie's Initial. "There's no need for everyone else to know I brought them here."

"Not until he answers some questions." She pointed a bony finger at Finn as she spoke. Finn couldn't help noticing how much thinner she had become. She seemed to be disappearing with age. He wondered if one day she'd wake up with no skin altogether: a walking, talking skeleton.

"He doesn't know anything," insisted Aunt Ev. "I brought him here because I felt sorry—"

"If you felt sorry for him, you'd leave him out of this! Let Will handle it his way. He knows what he's doing."

"You and *Will* seem awfully chummy lately. For someone who can't Future Travel, you sure seem to *think* you know what is going to happen. I wonder why."

Finn resisted the urge to speak. He wasn't trusting anyone, including himself. The voices below the choir loft were getting louder, and they sounded angry. While it was true he had known these people all his life, his friends and neighbors felt like complete strangers to him now. They were no longer individuals, they were a collective.

ISTA.

One thing he'd learned from Dad: All through history there were stories of good people, decent people, joining together to become a giant unstoppable force. People who would eventually regret what they had done in the name of whatever they called themselves. What were his neighbors capable of doing under that name? Finn recalled Aunt Ev's warning to

Gabi about being discovered: "If they see *you*, well, you don't want to know."

At the very least, they would send him to Albany, like Doc wanted. He couldn't let that happen. No one was going to stop him from getting to the top of Dorset Peak.

Billie was practically shaking with anger. "You don't know anything, Evelyn!" She spat the words out like poison.

"Why don't you enlighten me, Billie? What are you and Doc up to? You must be pleased Beth is out of the way now—maybe you can finally land him for yourself?"

"You're just like Beth! You can't see the importance of who we are. What we're meant to do!"

"Importance? You? Every day you find yourself slipping back and forth in time because you can't control what little power you have. What grand illusions are you harboring for yourself?"

Finn heard the others approaching behind, fumbling for keys to the locked panel in the floor, and more feet thrumming up the stairs behind the other door. They were trapped!

Well, he wasn't going to end up in Albany without a fight. He thrust both of his hands out in the air, palms out, and yelled, "Stop it! STOP ARGUING!"

Aunt Billie jumped backward in horror, her mouth open as if ready to scream. She slid down against the wall and cowered, shielding her face with her hands. Finn, Gabi, and Aunt Ev froze in confusion. Finn slowly lowered his arms and looked back at Aunt Ev questioningly, but she seemed as surprised at Billie's reaction as he was. Finn hadn't raised his hands in anger—he wasn't even making a fist—yet Aunt Billie was petrified. He felt awful. Scaring his great-aunts into thinking he was capable of violence was not part of his plan.

"I—I'm sorry. I'm sorry!"

The panel in the floor behind them began to open, and Finn knew he couldn't wait around to explain himself. They were out of time. He grabbed Gabi's hand and ran past the cowering Aunt Billie, down the stairs, toward the four illuminated letters at the bottom: EXIT.

CHAPTER 14

Shouting followed them once they were out in the open. Someone yelled "Stop!" and several lights popped on in the windows of small white houses surrounding the green. Finn heard a car door slam and an engine spring to life.

"We have to stay off the roads!" he hissed to Gabi.

They ran as fast as they could toward the golf course, then across the main road and into the woods.

"What happened?" Gabi panted as they pushed farther into the tree cover. "Why was she so afraid of you?"

"I don't know. I didn't do anything!" It didn't make sense. Finn could not figure out why he would appear so threatening to Aunt Billie.

They paused to catch their breath at the top of the hill.

"We have to get back to your house!" Gabi was poised to keep running.

Finn shook his head. "They're going to keep looking for us. My house is the first place they'll check." He held back the branches of a giant pine far enough to get a glimpse of the road. A car with high beams on was going by slowly. Finn was sure the members of ISTA would try to keep their search quiet, but they wouldn't give up easily.

"Do you think they called the police?" Gabi was peering out from behind his arm, trying to get a vantage point.

"They can't exactly call the police and say 'Hey, two kids crashed our secret time travel society meeting.'"

"What if the police were already there, Finn? Half the town was there!" Gabi sat down on a bed of pine needles and hugged her knees against her chest.

Finn felt a ripple of anger under his skin. For his entire life everyone had been keeping a secret from him. Well, not everyone. He made a mental tally in his mind. It wasn't half the town; maybe thirty-five people were there, tops.

"I don't think all of Dorset's in on it. They'll want to keep things quiet. Wait for us where they think we'll show up next."

He couldn't make out Gabi's face in the dark, but he heard her gasp. "Neither of our houses would be safe then. Even if they didn't see me, people know we're friends."

"Yeah. I think our best bet is to stay hidden and start the hike at sunup."

"But all our hiking gear is at my house . . . and the food and water and . . . you don't happen to have the trail guide on you, do you?"

Finn leaned hard against the nearest tree. "No." This was bad.

Gabi stood up and joined him, her back against the same tree. Her shoulder touched his arm. "Do you think Aunt Ev is really on your side? Maybe we can find her and ask for help."

"I'd like to think she is. But I can't be sure." Finn patted his pocket, feeling the crinkle of the paper and the curve of the stone. "And I don't think we can risk telling her about the tree."

"For a minute, I thought you were going to."

"I just wanted to see what her reaction would be. She obviously doesn't know about the portal. I think she suspects that Gran told me to do something, but she wasn't pressing it. Frankly, I'm not sure if she knows what she's doing."

Gabi nodded. "Yeah. Plus, she's a thief! I wonder how many things I've lost to time travelers. And ISTA will be watching her now, too."

"Did the Aunt Ev in the meeting look funny to you?"

"You mean the weird stuttery thing? No, but I couldn't get a good long look at her from my spot in the loft. Why?"

"I was just wondering." He didn't usually keep secrets from Gabi, but he kept the knowledge of the shimmer to himself. If you had asked him why at that moment, he wouldn't have had a good answer.

Another pair of headlights came from down below, lighting up the trees closest to the road.

Gabi reached for his hand. "We should hurry, keep moving into the woods."

They went as far as they could by moonlight. There was the stream that would become a full-on babbling brook in the rain, the circle of trees that Gabi always swore was a fairy ring, and the mounds of moss that would become the homes of little red forest lizards come spring. Back in third grade, whenever Gran was looking the other way, they'd tested their boundaries by going ever farther into these woods, until they knew the paths by heart. Gabi had always wanted to search for magical creatures, while Finn wanted to treat it like a scientific mission where they'd collect specimens to bring back for further study.

Gabi yawned into the night and Finn followed suit.

"We're somewhere behind Gran's now. We can stop." Finn slumped against a thick tree. He could see the boulder they used as base when they used to play hide and seek. He knew they were close to the trailhead.

Gabi looked over at him. "Do you remember how we used to play back here?"

"Yeah. You were always looking for fairies."

"And you were always looking for lizards. Can I ask you a question?" Her tone had changed. She looked away, busying herself with the lace of her sneaker. He wanted to say, *Please don't.*

"Why did you stop calling me?" Gabi's voice was quiet. "Why haven't you been inviting me over?"

This wasn't just a question. It was an asteroid on a collision path. "I've been texting you every day. I've been coming to your house."

"Only when I've been *making* you or you needed something." She turned to look directly at him. He found himself very grateful for the darkness.

"You were busy," he said. "You were with your *new friends.*"

The look on her face made Finn want to go back and edit his tone on those last two words. He shouldn't have said it like that.

She paused one heavy moment before she answered. "It was you who wasn't around. I reached out to them because I was tired of being alone—and guess what? They aren't all bad, Finn."

"Sebastian is a total reject."

"Sebastian is not my friend and you know it."

He didn't know it. That was just it. He had no idea anymore. "You know what I mean. We're not normal, Gabi. At least, I'm not. And you used to be like me."

Staring at his hands, he realized he had been picking at a hangnail on his thumb. It had started to bleed. In the moonlight the growing dot of blood looked black.

"Nobody is *normal*," said Gabi. "If you'd take the time to talk to anyone you'd see that. Everyone has something they're trying to figure out."

Finn pictured all the happy faces in the school hallways. It didn't seem possible they were focused on anything other than whom to torture next.

"You were always a loner, like me. We were loners together. Now you've gone and gotten so—so—well-adjusted." He was alternately sucking on his finger and thrusting it back in his pocket, trying not to let on that he was bleeding.

She balled her fists at her side. "I am *not* well-adjusted! What makes you think you get to be the expert on who is well-adjusted or not?"

Oh. She never even talked about Xavier. Finn knew about this part of her life—it just always seemed like ancient history to him. Something that occurred before she moved to Vermont, before they became Gabi and Finn.

"I'm sorry. I didn't mean it that way. It's just—well, you're so cool about it all. You're so good at dealing with it. You make people forget."

"Yeah, well, I don't forget and I am not good at dealing with it. What, like you talk about Faith all the time? You never even told me about the quarry!"

Finn felt her words in his gut. She was right.

"It's hard for me too," Gabi went on, picking at the hem of her jeans. "My brother died, my dad skipped town. I'm living in a tiny house that barely has enough air in it for me to breathe! And this town, you know everyone looks at my mom and assumes things. Like they think they know our whole story. It's not just Doc."

Dorset had always felt suffocating for Finn because his family was a favorite topic of gossip, but now Gabi was making him look at it in a whole new way. It was like she was turning and shaking a snow globe for him to peer into. It was stifling for her, too. He had never thought of her house as tiny, never considered it might be all Mrs. Rand could afford. He sat next to Gabi in stupefied silence.

She ran her hands through her short hair, and it stayed parted a little bit where her fingers had trailed through, like wet feathers. Finn felt as if he was looking at her, really looking at her, for the first time, as if she were brand-new to his life. Sitting there in the moonlight, she was the same, but somehow different. She was still small and wearing baggy clothes too big for her. She was wearing the same jeans and her favorite gray sweater that her mom had knitted for her. Maybe she didn't always wear it because it was her favorite. Maybe she didn't have much else. Why had he never thought about these things before?

An even worse idea entered his mind. What if she'd resented him all along for what he had? They never talked about their differences. He felt a dawning panic. Maybe childhood friendships meant nothing, maybe when you got older you somehow had to start all over. The stakes changed and you had to earn it all over again. You had to pay attention.

"Will you say something and stop staring at me?" Gabi snapped.

"Uh . . . I guess . . . we should talk about stuff more."

Talk about stuff? What he wanted to say was how much he admired her and wanted to be like her. How even though her life was as hard as his—harder—she had edges. She was real. He felt as if he was only defined by the empty spaces around him, by who wasn't there anymore. Faith's death, and Mom's leaving, and now Gran's death. He was an equation made entirely of missing variables. Unsolvable.

Gabi let out a frustrated snort.

"I'm sorry, Gabi. Really, I am."

"It's just that you act like you're the only person in the world who has to deal with people disappearing on you. You never even thought to talk to me about it. Me!"

She was right. He hadn't. "I'm an idiot."

"Well, now we agree on something." It was a dig, but her voice had softened.

There was something else he could talk to her about. His biggest secret.

"I've never told anyone this," Finn said quietly. "I don't really miss Faith, at least not the way everybody else does." There. He'd said it.

Her face gave him no indication of how she felt about that.

"It means I'm a terrible person, doesn't it?"

"No! You were so little. How *do* you miss her, exactly?" Gabi asked.

"I miss—me. Is that wrong? When she was here I was still Finn. I can remember that much."

"You're still Finn."

"No, I'm not. To everyone in town, I'm the little drowned girl's brother. I'm the constant unwelcome reminder. My dad can't even look at me anymore. He looks past me at whatever is behind me, like it's more interesting. Mom probably left because of me."

"You know that's not true, right?"

"I don't know that. I don't know anything."

"Well, I know. I know who you are too. You are my best friend." He was happy she said it. Even though, in light of all her new friends, this still felt like something that could be taken from him at any time.

"When does life feel normal again after people leave you, or after someone just goes and dies?"

She paused before she answered. "It doesn't. It doesn't go back to the way it was, I mean. It's just a new life. *That* starts to feel normal."

"How?" He honestly wanted to know. It had been three weeks since Mom had disappeared and nothing was returning to any semblance of livable. His family had lost Faith almost ten years ago and everyone was still wounded, including him. "I don't know, just one day it happens." A small smile began to form at the corners of her mouth, a memory. Finn wished that memory could play for him like a movie. "For my mom and me, it was just laughing at something stupid. Something totally not funny, but it made us laugh anyway. It was the first time I had felt okay in a long time."

Finn tried to imagine him and Dad laughing over anything. It didn't seem like it would ever be a possibility again. But Mom—Mom would laugh with him.

They both sat in silence against the tree for a moment. Gabi spoke first. "We should take turns getting some sleep."

"You go ahead. I'll be fine. I'm not as tired as I sound."

"Are you sure? You haven't slept much at all since your gran—"

Finn stopped her before she would have to search for a better word than *died*. "I'm fine. I can handle it." His voice was full of false confidence that she accepted for truth.

Gabi balled up her hoodie and used it as a pillow. "Okay, but wake me if you need to switch."

Finn sat there, listening to the sounds of the woods. In the distance he could hear the muted hoot of an owl, and if he listened closely he could make out the scurrying of small creatures through leaves. It didn't take longer than three or four minutes before Gabi's breathing slowed, and Finn knew he was alone with the night.

CHAPTER 15

He must have fallen asleep for a little bit. It was more like a half-sleep, filled with questions disguising themselves as dreams. In one dream he felt he had the answer to everything in the universe. He could see inside people's minds, or maybe it was hearts, and he could see the impressions he left with them. The feelings he inspired in them became visible like stars. The good ones were iridescent and swelling, growing larger and brighter. The bad ones were small and dark, contracting like a vacuum in space.

In his dream, he knew it was important to stack up as many big shiny stars as possible. It was the secret to everything—these little moving, expanding and contracting stars.

That was all he could remember when he woke.

It was still dark, but he could tell it was that time

of night that was just about to give way to morning. The sun would be up soon. The first thing that sprang to life was the ache in his heart. It was always present in the morning, when he'd have to remind himself that Mom was no longer there. And now, he had Gran to add to the black hole inside his chest. He began to mentally catalog what he had discovered in the last forty-eight hours. He would stick to the facts. The facts were easier to deal with.

1. The women in his family could time travel.

2. His town had a secret society to protect the timeline—though he still had no idea from whom.

3. Gran had been in charge of ISTA.

4. Dorset marble had properties yet to be discovered or understood, or at least Aunt Ev thought so.

5. People moved like spliced film when they were Traveling too close to their Initial, and their Initial shimmered when the Traveling version was close by.

That last part was the most interesting to him, mostly because nobody besides himself appeared to know about the shimmer. Gabi hadn't seen it, and Aunt Ev hadn't brought it up either—though maybe she was just so used to it that she neglected to mention it.

He leaned forward on his knees, giving his back a

rest from the uncomfortable tree trunk that his spine had practically fused to during the night. Its bark looked like the striated backs of his hands when he studied them up close. In the half-awake moments of dawn he had the weird feeling that his skin was just softer bark. Under a microscope everything looks related.

He took a deep breath. He reached into his right front pocket and pulled out Gran's shopping-list-turned-warning and Aunt Ev's grounding stone.

Gran had said she would be back.

"How about now, Gran?" he whispered into the twilight. "I could use some answers."

But how many answers would Gran have? It seemed that at some point she had realized Doc had deceived her. Did she know about Billie and Doc? He still wasn't sure what Aunt Billie had to do with all of this either.

At any rate, Gran -5 was missing some key facts, and that worried him more than anything. If Gran had gone back in time five years to get help from herself, why didn't she tell herself everything? Why did Gran -5 tell him to trust Doc? And which Gran changed her mind?

There were so many questions and no one around to answer them. His mouth was dry and his neck was stiff with cold and lack of proper sleep. He heard Gabi stir next to him.

"Well, I'm not sure I slept at all." Gabi croaked out the words.

"Me neither."

"You did. I heard you snore." She shook out her makeshift pillow and put it back on over her sweater.

"I did not!"

"Yes, you did. I was looking at you and your mouth was wide open. I'm surprised nothing made a home in it overnight."

Finn smacked his lips together and gulped a few times. "It kind of tastes like something did."

"I'd give anything for some Earl Grey with five packets of sugar." She pulled the hood up over her head and leaned against the tree with him. "No one came for us. Do you think they gave up searching?"

"No. I think they'll expect us to get hungry and come out of hiding sooner or later. I don't think anyone suspects we're going up the mountain."

A rather plump robin was welcoming the morning with more energy than the rest of the forest. Finn looked at it with appreciation, feeling the need to make an enthusiastic move of his own. "Let's start. The sun is almost up and we can get ahead of any leaf peepers—or anyone else."

Approaching the trailhead meant approaching Gran's house. Finn was afraid of two things: who would be watching her house, and whether he could keep it together in front of Gabi. He didn't want to think of seeing Gran the way he had, lifeless and staring at nothing. The safest place in his world no longer felt safe.

Gran's house had the audacity to look exactly the same as before. Finn had an impulse to throw a rock and break one of the upstairs windows. Birds continued to eat at Gran's bird feeder, and Finn wondered who would fill it now. He wanted to tell them to ration the seed, that it was special. It was from Gran and there'd never be more.

There was a finality to Gran's disappearance. One he hadn't been old enough to feel for Faith right away. What if Mom—? No. No time to think of that now.

"You okay?" Gabi sidled up next to him and looked through the trees toward Gran's house.

"I'm fine. Let's make sure we stay far behind the tree line. They're going to be watching her house, too."

She grabbed his hand and squeezed it softly. It was her way of saying she knew. She knew this was hard for him and she knew saying anything would only make it harder. Finn squeezed back.

They plodded on, making their own path through the woods where there was none. Their footsteps in the leaves sounded too loud to Finn in the early dawn. They entered the trailhead about four hundred feet up from the parking area. He couldn't see any cars from where they were, but that didn't mean they weren't hidden around the bend. The trail was wide here, wide enough to drive a car down. Finn knew it got narrower and narrower.

"We still don't have a map," Gabi said.

"I read part of the trail guide last night before Aunt Ev showed up. I think I can remember some of it. The quickest trail to the top is the one with orange blazes." The truth was he wasn't very sure of that, but in reassuring Gabi he also reassured himself.

Gabi gave him a smile that was more wistful than courageous. "Well, you follow a trail up and then you come back down. How hard can it be?"

"Ha ha," he said.

"Still, it's the only plan we have, right?" she said.

"Okay. The guide said the bottom of the trail allows for vehicles and snowmobiles, but it's only like this for a little bit. That's always about as far as

I went when I was little and walked with my mom. She said the higher elevations would be too hard for me back then. Not, like, recently, or anything." He didn't want Gabi to think he was a total weakling.

He had been old enough to handle this hike for a while now. Yet he had never shown any interest in going with Mom. If he had, he would know the trail. He'd probably even know where to find the tree. Mom probably had favorite spots along the way. All that information would have been useful. He'd like to Travel back in time and tell himself to take more interest.

The ground was carpeted with dead leaves. The ruts from last winter's snowmobile traffic were now long narrow puddles from the rainstorms, but it was easy enough to stay in the middle of the trail and keep out of the mud.

Gabi was on the same wavelength. "Don't get your feet wet. We're going to have a hard enough time as it is in these flimsy sneakers."

They plodded on, Gabi in front and Finn following close behind. He was the faster walker and figured it was better to let her set the pace.

Finn studied the long grooves in the mud. Some were fresh dirt bike tracks. Bikers must also use this early part of the trail for fun.

He bumped into Gabi, nearly tumbling over her. "Ouch! A little warning before braking next time, okay?"

"Sorry. It's just—there's a fork." She gestured in front of her.

Sure enough, the path in front of them divided into two.

"What did the guidebook say?" Gabi asked.

"It didn't. I'm sure of it. There wasn't anything about a fork at this elevation. We're supposed to keep traveling straight along the trail until we see a clearing and then an old hunting cabin."

"Well, the fork is here. Is there a blaze or a cairn anywhere?" They looked for something that would tell them which way to go. None of the trees were marked with an orange blaze, and there was no tottering stack of stones either.

"Maybe it isn't marked because it's one of those that meet up with each other farther in," Gabi offered. "Maybe it doesn't matter which way you go."

Finn studied both choices and they looked exactly the same. It was too early in the hike for setbacks. He began to second-guess himself. Maybe he was remembering the trail guide wrong.

"We can go right, and if we don't find the clearing we'll come back to this point and try again," Gabi offered.

"I feel like it's left. We should go left."

Gabi didn't disagree but she looked skeptical. "Well, let's mark it." She looked around on the ground and found enough stones to make a small cairn at the base of a skinny tree.

Finn knew enough to know this was what hikers did. You needed a way to mark where you'd been, so you could find it again.

They went left at Finn's urging. He took the lead, promising not to walk too fast.The trail narrowed to only a few feet wide and began to slope up. The woods became winter-quiet, like the birds weren't planning on following.

The trail was poorly maintained. Maybe it had been "well marked" years ago—Finn realized that he hadn't checked the publication date of the trail guide—but so far he hadn't seen a single blaze on a tree. He wasn't sure they were going the right way and he had a horrible fear that this would keep happening. They'd keep on reaching unmarked forks. They might never be able to find the right route to the summit, or even worse, the right route back down. Finn kept that little concern to himself.

He focused on the the immediate goal. "Assuming we do find the tree . . ." he began.

"Yeah . . ." Gabi was still walking behind him. Finn didn't want to turn and see her face yet.

"You know a portal *goes* somewhere."

"Or some*when*."

"Right, and who knows if it will even work. But if it does, well—I need to go alone." The sound of her footsteps stopped abruptly behind him. He forced himself to turn around and face her.

"Seriously? We've been over this. You're not going without me!" She set her shoulders and started walking again.

Finn stayed squarely in her way, unmoving. "We don't know where it goes, Gabi. I don't know what I'll find there. I don't even know if I'll make it back."

"We'll make it back. Together." She maneuvered around him and stubbornly took the lead. This was her way of saying she had already won the argument.

Finn did not follow. "Someone needs to stay behind to tell my dad what happened." *In case I don't come back. In case—*

Gabi turned back to glare at him. "No."

"Gabi, I have to do this. It's my family and my problem. I'm not going to let you get hurt or lost because of me."

Her face softened. She placed her hand on his arm. "Nothing is going to happen to me."

"There's no guarantee of that. You and I know that better than anyone, Gabi."

Her eyes softened. She knew, just like he did. Remainders must be careful.

"Listen, if anything does happen, couldn't your aunt Ev go back in time and stop us? Think about it—she obviously rehearsed that entry into the church. She knew where everyone would be looking, right down to the second on her giant watch! She can redo things."

"I don't think it works that way, Gabi. If it did, why is Gran dead? Why is Mom missing at all? Why didn't Aunt Ev know that Aunt Billie would come back? I don't think infinite do-overs are a possibility."

The doubt he was casting landed straight on her shoulders. He saw her bravado fade, and she actually appeared to shrink a few inches.

"Even one do-over would be enough, wouldn't it?" she said. "And we know at least one is possible, because last night Aunt Ev said I wasn't there before."

Finn shook his head. "I don't think it's something we should count on. If my family could just go back and change everything that goes wrong, our lives should have been a whole lot easier up till now. Nothing bad would've happened to any of us." Mom would be safe. Faith would never have drowned.

The toe of Gabi's sneaker worried at the carpet of dead leaves. He could see that she was realizing the problem with her logic. "But I'm here for a reason this time! I have to be . . ." Her voice trailed off. Finn felt bad for ruining her theory. He wasn't sure if her eyes were welling up with tears or if the glint of the sun through the leaves was playing a trick. He couldn't understand why this was so important to her.

He also couldn't ignore the growing seed of knowledge inside him, that the danger was far more than either of them could fully understand. It occurred to him, a little too late, that he needed Gabi to have her usual courage. Instead, he had gone and infected her with his doubt.

"Can we agree to disagree till we find it?" It was a stalling mechanism, but it was all he had. He would stop her once they got to the peak.

She gave him a halfhearted smile. "Yes. That's a good plan."

He was sure she had no intention of listening to him. He knew he'd have to find the tree first.

"Speaking of which, we've been walking along this trail for half an hour now and we've yet to see a clearing," Gabi said. "I think we made the wrong turn. I think we should go back."

"It's possible we just haven't hit it yet."

"We should head back to the fork and choose the other way." She turned and began walking back down the path, as if Finn would automatically follow.

Resentment boiled up inside of him. No one ever let him have control, including Gabi.

He called after her, "Stop it, Gabi! I've been asked by *my* family to do this. Mine! I've asked you to come along, but this is one time you can't be in charge."

She spun around and looked up at him, her mouth opened in a perfect 'o' of shock. After a moment, she recovered her composure and walked back up the trail till they were face to face. Finn was staring down into Gabi's intense gaze. She was on her tiptoes with both arms rigid at her sides. Finn began to get nervous and wondered how quickly he could duck a punch from Gabi. She was small but fierce.

"Don't think this is just your fight, Finn. I'm already involved. I know your secret, and I'm the one

ISTA will come after if you don't come home."

Finn exhaled. "Let's try another ten minutes up this trail. If we don't find the clearing then we can turn around and go your way. Fair?" he asked.

"Okay, but I'm setting my alarm." She pulled her phone out of her pocket. "When it goes off, we at least think about turning around, okay?"

Finn didn't answer. He took the lead again.

She muttered something under her breath that Finn couldn't hear. It didn't matter. He felt sure he was on the right trail.

CHAPTER 16

With every step Finn took he expected to see more sunlight filtering through the trees. He waited for the clearing. Down couldn't be the right direction, it had to be up. He quickened his pace—he had to cover as much ground as possible before Gabi made him turn around.

"I know what you're doing," Gabi panted behind him. "Just because you're going faster doesn't make it the right trail."

"I'm sorry. I just need to see around this bend in the path ahead. We can stop here and take a breather if you want."

Gabi plopped down right in the middle of the path and put her head between her knees. "I wish we had water."

"I know." He agreed even though he wasn't all

that thirsty. He was done feeling hopeless. He was ready to keep on climbing. In fact, he was sure he could do it for days if he had to. Nothing was going to stop him now that he was here. His legs itched to keep going. It was clear hers needed a rest though. She began rubbing her calves with her hands.

She gestured for him to go. "Hurry up ahead. I'll wait here. If there's no clearing we have to go back to the fork and go my way."

That was all the permission he needed. Finn bolted up the trail, the leaves crackling beneath his feet and his thigh muscles burning as the trail became steeper and steeper. As he turned the corner, he saw it. Dark leaves parted to show a flash of bright green ferns.

It was there.

A clearing.

He rushed ahead and let the morning sun hit his face full force. The field was full of new growth. It was like he had found a patch of newborn spring hiding away from autumn.

Below him, he could hear Gabi's phone alarm ring out faintly. He smiled and turned back to the trail.

"Finn? Are you there?" There was fear in her voice. "Please say you're there." She was trudging back up the trail looking for him.

He ran back around the corner and beamed a smile at her.

"Really?" she asked.

"Really. It's the right trail."

ooo

"I will never again doubt the Mighty Finn!" Gabi twirled in the sun, arms out and laughing.

"Yeah, don't make promises you can't keep!" Finn laughed. They weren't lost. This moment of victory felt good, and he was grateful to her for acknowledging it. It also meant he could trust his instincts. It meant the cards weren't all stacked against them.

"It's too pretty not to stop." She waded into the ferns and proceeded to sit cross-legged in the middle of the clearing. Her head barely cleared the green fronds. She motioned for him to come sit next to him. "The ground here is dry."

As welcoming as the image was, he did not want to stop again.

"Just for a minute. Consider it a vitamin D break." She tilted her face up to the sun.

"Now I know you're spending too much time in Mr. Schuman's outdoors club."

He followed the path of bent ferns she had made and sat down. The sun did feel good on his face.

"So what would you change?" he asked.

"Change?"

"In time. History. What if we could change anything—everything!—once we find the tree?"

"I'd pack water," Gabi deadpanned.

"Okay, obviously that. But seriously, what big things?" Finn asked.

"Oh. I don't know." She sounded like she did know.

"You could stop your brother from going overseas," he suggested.

Gabi grabbed a handful of ferns in her right hand and began to grind them into a pile of light green mulch. "Maybe. I mean—I miss Xavi like crazy. Of course I do. I would want him back in a heartbeat. It's just, well, it doesn't seem like it's all that simple, that's all."

"Of course it is. It would just take some planning. Figuring out what the key moments were. We could do it!"

"You're not getting it."

If there was anything Finn hated being accused of, it was being dense. "But—"

"Think, Finn! We wouldn't be who we are now! I might never leave New York. I'd never move here. Bringing him back would change everything."

Finn didn't have a rebuttal for that. She was right. They might end up not knowing each other.

He didn't like to imagine a world where he didn't know Gabi. His whole life would be different. *He* would be different.

Every single action has consequences. He could imagine some of them, but there were probably a million others he couldn't even guess at. Finn felt like he needed some complex software to figure it all out. It made his head hurt.

"I don't know how they live like this. Mom, Gran, my aunts . . . having to think about every possible outcome before they do anything. It could make you lose your mind."

"But that's what they were stopping. Aunt Ev said ISTA is all about keeping the timeline safe from changes, right?"

"Still, it's a nearly impossible task. Anything you do, back in time, could change something." He stretched out his legs, realizing how sore they were from all the walking. "Do you remember when I tried to teach you chess?"

Gabi laughed. "Yes! Don't say *try* like I didn't get it. I got it. I just hated it." She went back to massaging the blood flow back into her legs.

"Do you remember why you hated it? What you said to me?" Finn knelt down on the ground in front of her.

"Yeah. It all got too annoying when you told me *entire games are predestined by opening moves.*" She put on her special Finn-mocking voice. Somehow she always made him sound British. "I forgot what you called them."

"Gambits. People make a specific first move, and then the rest of the game plays out in a certain way. The same games have been replayed over centuries."

"There is no point in playing a game where I can't be original." She smiled at the memory and then the smile disappeared. She seemed to forget about her sore legs. "Oh—you think this is like a chess game, being played over and over?"

"If we go with my theory, then yes. Each time Gran or Mom, or whoever, tries to change the timeline, they open with a different gambit and watch how the chain of events plays out. Except the chessboard has limits. It's a finite square. The other player can only do a few different things with their pieces.

In real life, people can do way too many unpredictable things. Every decision we make will change the course of the timeline." He placed the heel of his palms over both eyes as if to give his senses a break. "There are too many permutations to even consider. There's no point."

"I don't know. Some people are very predictable." She lay down in the ferns, cradling her head in her arms. "Maybe with those people, you could bank on them doing the same thing each time, staying inside the square."

Finn lay down on his back next to her. "I can't think of anybody who would do the same *wrong* thing, not if they knew the consequences."

"I think some people would. Even if they had the chance to do better they still wouldn't take it. I can also think of a few people who would always do the right thing."

She didn't say who. She was staring at a hawk lazily circling high overhead, riding those invisible air spirals they somehow know how to find.

"Maybe this isn't really all that weird," she said. "I mean on some level, everyone is a product of choices that were made before they could remember, before they were even born. We are who we are because we live here, but we didn't choose that. Our parents did, and in your case your parents' parents and so on. Our lives are built on the decisions of others."

He couldn't argue with that, though it seemed unfair that so much of his own identity was outside his control. "Maybe if your brother didn't die, then—"

"Finn, not now. Okay? I've played that game lots of times. I know you have, too. It's not like we don't have lots of practice at this."

"Practice?"

"Well, in a way, we've both been time travelers for a long time already. Haven't we? I mean, that's all you do after you lose someone. You keep going back, over and over again."

Finn nodded slowly. "Or you bring the ghost of them forward—Travel them to now. So you can just talk to them, show them things."

"Yes." She looked at him in surprise, like she couldn't believe someone else understood. They were connected again, by something deep and ancient. It felt like the beginning of a universe. She turned away first and it was almost a relief.

"It certainly is a safer way to time travel," he offered.

"I don't know about that. You can't build a future,

or even a present, by talking to the past all the time," she said. "Let's take thirty more seconds to watch the sky and feel the sun. We won't see it again for a while."

As they lay there, backbones against the hard earth, the sunlight glowing amber behind their closed eyelids, he was filled with gratitude that Gabi was there. She made him feel solid. When he was with her he wasn't floating around without edges. He was grounded.

CHAPTER 17

The next landmark in the trail guide was supposed to be the hunter's cabin. It was common for mountains to have one or two cabins shared by hunters who prefer something more than a tent. Finn had never gone far enough up Dorset Peak to see one, though.

The structure in front of them was not the quaint, cozy cabin he expected. Black, tar-papered and sinister looking, it rose out of the mountain like a thorn. Modern sashed windows jutted out of the dirty tarpaper like cataract-covered eyes, trying to see who might be thinking about trespassing.

Finn and Gabi froze. The building made Finn wonder what kind of hunting the occupants did.

"That place is freaky looking." Gabi's feet stayed rooted to the trail. The cabin lay a good thirty feet in front of them. "Do you think anyone is in it?"

She looked up at the roof and Finn followed her gaze. A narrow stovepipe chimney jutted out the top at an odd angle. There wasn't any smoke drifting out the top.

"If they are they don't have a fire on."

She pursed her lips. "Let's keep going. This place gives me the creeps. It looks like the home of a serial killer."

"Come on, Gabi. This is taking much longer than we thought and we might be up here overnight. We don't have the proper provisions. You said so yourself. There could be food or water in there."

"Yeah, or victims hanging from the rafters! I'd rather take my chances. *Please*, let's go."

"You can stay out here if you like. I'll only be a minute. I'll go around the other side and see if there's an open door."

Without waiting for an answer, Finn slowly began to make his way closer to the cabin. He watched the windows but didn't see any movement. As he got closer he realized that didn't mean anything. The windows were so dirty he wouldn't be able to see through one even if his nose was pressed against it.

He edged around the cabin to get a view of the only door. It was at an unnatural height and there were no stairs leading up to it. It would take a big step to get up there, and that wasn't even the most unsettling thing about it.

Right over the bleak-looking mismatched door, nailed unceremoniously between the roof's apex and the entryway, was a rotting animal skull. It still had some meat on it and flies were buzzing around it in a frenzy. Finn stopped in his tracks and tried to make out what that creature might have been. Its two hollowed-out eye cavities stared ahead in perpetual shock.

A hand grabbed Finn's upper arm hard. He nearly swung a fist before realizing it was Gabi.

"Whoa! It's just me—What the . . ." She had noticed it. Finn figured it was probably a fox skull, or maybe a deer, based on the size.

"That is disgusting!" Gabi said. "Let's leave, please. There won't be anything we want in here. This is the scariest place I've ever seen."

Finn could not tear himself away. It was as if he'd been plucked from reality and placed in a dreamscape. As if he'd dreamed of this building before and now he was being given the opportunity to explore it in real-life detail. Only when he searched his memory for it, there was nothing there.

He moved closer to the makeshift door and did his best to listen. Sometimes when someone is being quiet so as not to be heard, you can hear their efforts.

Finn listened for small furtive movements. Nothing.

Still, he couldn't just go barging in. He raised his hand and knocked hard on a small patch of smooth wood that didn't have nails bent this way and that. A cluster of birds flew up from the nearby underbrush in alarm.

Gabi put her hands over her ears, as if muffling the sound of his knock would somehow make them safer. She glanced quickly to the left and right and then back at him.

Finn knocked harder this time and the door gave way. It wasn't clear if he'd dislodged or if someone had unlatched it from inside.

Gabi stepped back. "I don't like this."

Finn peered inside, and it took a second for his eyes to adjust to the darkness. Motes of dust cascaded down sunbeams filtering in through the filthy windows. Something small, maybe a mouse, scuttled across the room at the far corner. A rusty heating stove anchored the other end of that tilted metal chimney they'd seen from outside. Squatting in the middle of the room, a wooden sawhorse table filled the majority of the space. It was covered in the unmistakable stains of dried blood.

Finn reassured himself that this discovery was normal. It was, after all, a hunter's cabin.

He took one step in and realized there was a platform over his head. A space that he couldn't see into from the floor level.

"Hello? Is anyone here?" he called.

No one answered. Even the mouse had stopped moving.

Gabi had not followed him inside. She was outside the door. "Is there water?"

"Still looking. I don't think anyone has been here recently. It's hard to tell."

He spotted a ladder that led to the platform. As he examined it, Gabi entered and followed his footsteps across the mismatched floorboards.

"I don't think we'll find a stocked fridge in here," she said.

"There's fresh footprints on the floor." Finn gestured at the ladder. "But there's a full layer of dust on the ladder rungs."

"So whoever uses this place doesn't sleep here. Good for them. I wouldn't either. Let's go."

"In a minute." Taking a deep breath, he tested the first rung of the ladder with his weight, then climbed up to the second.

The loft was empty. He let out his breath in relief. He assumed it was for sleeping, since no grown human being could stand up straight in that small a space. There were some old dingy blankets up there, a broken hurricane lamp—and a retro-looking red and white travel cooler. Could they be that lucky? He grabbed the handle and tilted it back, and inside he found three bottled waters. Unopened.

"Gabi! I found water!"

"Really?"

"Yeah, they're warm. Beggars can't be choosers right?" He tossed one to her. "Ration it, there's only three."

She took a gulp, capped the bottle, and put it in the front double pocket of her hoodie. "I don't even care that it's not cold."

Finn began to descend from the loft. As he held onto the ladder he realized that it wasn't dust on the rungs, but soot. Whoever used this cabin let their lamps and candles burn all night long. Finn couldn't blame them. He wouldn't be caught dead in this cabin after dark. A shiver shook him as he realized how creepy that saying was.

"Let's hurry," Gabi said. "I don't want to run into whoever hung the fresh skull, okay?"

"Excellent point. Go be lookout."

Gabi seemed all too happy to leave and disap peared out the front door by jumping down its large front step. From his vantage point it looked like she disappeared entirely.

Finn hopped off the ladder and walked around carefully, looking at the cobwebs and searching for any other signs that someone had been here. A small shelf over the stove held two blue speckled metal bowls that looked older than him by thirty years at least. A daddy long-legs was sprawled out on the wall above them. Next to that were the remnants of a dead plant in a dingy terracotta pot. All that was left of the plant were some leggy white roots that jutted out from the soil.

Gabi peered in from the front door, only her head and shoulders visible. "Hurry up!" she hissed.

Gabi opened the door wider, and as the sun swept across the floorboards Finn could see the varying footprints in the dust. Theirs were the freshest. The other set looked similar to theirs but without the ridges in the rubber sneaker soles. Those prints appeared normal in some areas, yet in others they looked elongated, as if the foot was being dragged. In the corner they disappeared altogether and reappeared a few feet away. Like stutter-steps. Like a Traveler's.

Was the skull nailer someone from ISTA? Fear slinked up Finn's spine at the thought of Doc and Aunt Billie being three steps ahead of him.

No, he was leaping to wild conclusions.

"Finn! Come on!"

He took one last look around. He woudn't tell her about the strange footprints. There was no reason to scare her now.

It's not like I begrudged them the water—goodness knows they need it far more than I do—but you go through all the trouble of packing certain things. It's the devil to lose them.

Okay, fine. You caught me. I would have brought them more, but I can only take so much with me. It's not easy Traveling such distances.

This isn't the most comfortable lodging, but it will do for now. Eons know I've stayed in much worse. It's not like I'll be sleeping anyway. I have to keep watch and be ready. Play my part.

The skull wasn't meant for them. It was meant to scare me off. It didn't do its job. There is no way to get rid of me. That is something my adversary will not understand for a long, long time.

So busy trying to control the world, shaping the timeline, that you can't even see the truth in front of your face!

Well, I'm not scared.

I can't be scared off when I've already seen the worst that could happen.

CHAPTER 18

"Why would anyone nail a skull to the door like that?" Gabi was still unnerved as they set off again.

"Probably to scare nosey hikers and leaf peepers away. They're hunters, after all."

"It's disgusting and cruel! I wish we could take another route down." Gabi was walking faster than she had at any point so far. Finn couldn't blame her. He wanted to put distance between them and the cabin, too.

The trail did nothing but climb at an impossible angle from the cabin on up. The trees wrapped over themselves and created an impenetrable ceiling of leaves that filtered out the sun. Finn couldn't say he minded the shade. The path was now so steep that each step was beginning to take a toll on his legs and the exertion made him warm. He made a walking stick from a downed branch and found himself relying on it more and more. The idea of telescoping poles sounded really good to him right about now. And he wasn't the only one struggling; he could hear Gabi's ragged breathing behind him.

They gave up conversation. Finn was glad because he didn't want to sound breathless. Instead of focusing on his screaming leg muscles, he looked down at the ground. The trail looked different at this altitude. It was no longer a carpet of brown and rusty leaves, but a newer green and yellow layer of teardrop-shaped ones. He should probably know what they were called. Aspens came to mind, but he couldn't be sure. He looked up at the surrounding trees. They all looked the same to him.

It would have helped if Gran and Mom had at least told him what kind of tree he should look for at the summit.

When he was little he and Gran would take long walks, and she would name each tree for him. He couldn't remember anything specific about those days, only that the sun was always shining when they were together.

Gabi's footsteps behind him slowed and stopped.

"You okay? You need to rest a bit?"

"No. I—yeah. Sorry."

"No, it's okay." The truth of it was he needed the rest, too. He sat down on the green and yellow leaf carpet and let the blood rush back into his legs.

"It's—it's all so steep!" Gabi was still fighting for her breath. "I keep thinking it will level out a bit whenever I see a turn up ahead and then no, it's just more straight up."

She pulled out her water bottle and took a big long gulp this time. Finn had planned to share the extra bottle between them, but now he thought he'd give it to her. He took a small sip of his own.

He checked the time on his phone. It was bad. Four hours had passed and they were nowhere near the summit. At least it didn't look like it. How could he even tell? If they were only halfway they'd never get back down again before dark.

Gabi seemed to read his mind. "Okay, I'm ready. Let's go." She struggled to stand on shaky legs.

"Have you noticed?" she said as they trudged forward. "There are no birds up here."

Finn hadn't noticed. "Yeah, come to think of it there are no chirping crickets either."

"It feels different up here." She crossed her arms

around her middle.

"Well, it's colder."

"It's something else too."

"What?"

"You'll make fun of me for it."

"No I won't."

"Yes, you will, but I'm going to say it anyway. There's something big and alive up here. It takes up all the space. It's like I can feel the mountain breathing below my feet."

"I think you're channeling Aunt Ev now." Finn tried to hide the amusement in his voice.

"See? You're so predictable."

"No, no. I can see how you'd feel that way. I feel something, too. I just don't attribute it to anything mystical. It could be magnetic fields, or the effect of a quick atmospheric change on the human brain . . ."

Gabi was shaking her head while staring up at the trees, the ones that Finn figured might be aspens. "Call it whatever you want. I know it's something different. Bigger. Magical."

He wanted to agree with her. If people could time travel, why couldn't mountains breathe under your feet? But he couldn't make that illogical leap, not even for Gabi. That's not what he was about. And somewhere in the back of his brain something primal was telling him that when your world has completely fallen apart, you need to hang on to who you are.

Finn was a scientist.

So he offered what a scientist could. "Quantum mechanics is the closest thing to real magic I've read about. Subatomic particles have laws they're governed by, and if the universe has hidden laws that rule the very smallest of objects, well, it can sort of look like magic."

He could practically see Gabi's mind tune him out through her glazed-over eyes.

With an arched eyebrow, Gabi said, "Well, we now know time travel is real, but can you explain it? Does it fit into your science books?"

"No, not yet. But I bet I'll be able to figure it out in time. Everything is eventually explained by science."

"Yeah, now *that's* the part I'm not so sure about."

They walked on in silence—the only sound their labored breathing, as they tried to get to the top as fast as they could. Now that Gabi had brought it to his attention, Finn missed the sound of the birds.

ooo

The trail was a relentless climb with no views, no waterfalls, no clearings of any sort after the hunting cabin, only lots of unidentifiable forks in the trail. Some ended in dead ends that forced them to go back down to the point where they diverged. Those were the moments that filled Finn with the most doubt. What if one of those dead ends had once led to the portal? What if the trail Mom intended him to take was now grown over, blocked by a fallen tree and left to nature to fill back in?

"Gran didn't say anything about what the tree looks like?" panted Gabi. She was having a hard time, stumbling more, wheezing a little. Finn was afraid to ask her if she was okay.

"No. She just said we had to go to the summit."

"Are you sure she said the summit?"

"Yes, I'm sure."

That was a lie. He wasn't sure of anything anymore. It wasn't like he had been in the best frame of mind while talking to Gran. He tried hard to remember. He could have sworn she said it was at the top, but that might be his own memory filling in the blanks. Was the top the same as the summit? There was the horrible possibility that it was lower on the trail and they had somehow missed it. The droplets of sweat on his forehead grew cold. It was impossible to look at every tree along the way and see if there was something different about it. Surely, Mom had picked a tree that would stand out. He hoped it stood like a climber's flag at the peak, glowing and obvious.

The real truth was he had no idea.

"What if we don't find it?" said Gabi.

"Then we stay up here till we do," he answered.

A long moment passed before she weakly responded, farther behind him now. "I need to stop again. I'm sorry."

His heart sank. Gabi looked exhausted. Her face was bright red and her hair was plastered to her forehead. She sank to her knees. He had been pushing them hard in the last hour. Maybe too hard. They had been on the mountain for a full six hours.

Gabi looked like she was ready to give up. Finn felt a little panicked at the thought. She was right, he couldn't do this alone. He needed her.

"Yeah. Let's stop." Finn tried to sound upbeat. He sounded unnatural and he knew it. They might as well take five minutes—there was no way they'd get off this mountain in daylight now. They could take thirty if they wanted. They both realized it, even if they didn't want to say it out loud.

"We have to be close to the peak by now."

The air had gotten colder and the trees were different again. Some type of sparse-looking evergreen, their lower branches covered in bright green mossy stuff that hung like tattered clothing.

Gabi took off one of her sneakers and as she did, Finn could see a bright red bloom of blood along the bottom of her sock.

"Aw man, Gabi. You okay?"

"Blisters popped a while back. These aren't the best hiking shoes. I'll be all right, I just wish I had something to wrap around them." She tugged at the bottom of the t-shirt she was wearing under her sweater. It took Finn a moment before he realized what she was trying to do. She wasn't giving up. She was digging in. She was going to rip up part of her shirt for bandages.

He reached into his pocket and pulled out his keychain. "It's a penknife. It opens."

"Thanks." She made quick work of it.

"Gabi, I—"

"It's okay, Finn. It's just a little bit of blood. I got this." She smiled at him, but it didn't reach her eyes. She was able to get three long strips of cloth from the bottom of her shirt that she wound around her foot.

"Are you going to be able to keep walking on that?"

The look she gave him did not fill him with much confidence. "Let's hope so." Finn watched her struggle to get her sneaker back on over the bloody sock and makeshift bandages.

Then they both heard it—the sound of something large coming up the path behind them. Instinctively, Finn grabbed Gabi's hand and yanked her off the trail before she even had time to stand. She stumbled after him into the trees. The underbrush here was nearly nonexistent. The trees would be their only cover, so they'd have to move quickly. Finn ducked underneath a branch and got a face full of drippy green moss.

He and Gabi crouched behind a small rise of land only about fifteen feet from the trail. They were still very much out in the open when they saw him.

A huge outline of a man reached the crest of the trail. It was Mr. Wells. Finn could tell from his expensive oiled barn coat. It wasn't park ranger's gear—it was Ray Wells all right, dressed posh as usual, like a leaf peeper up for a country weekend.

ISTA had found them.

Mr. Wells unbuttoned his coat, knelt down with one knee on the hard packed dirt of the trail, and pulled a radio from his belt.

"They're up here." He then spotted something on the ground and reached for it. It was Finn's pen knife keychain. Gabi had dropped it when Finn dragged her into the trees.

Finn could hear a crackled male response come from the radio, but it was unintelligible.

"Nah, I didn't see them, but it looks like they ran when they heard me. Has to be them. I won't let them get any farther."

Wells pushed the radio into a pocket of his tan canvas belt. As he stood up and faced their direction, he placed both hands on his waist, flaring his jacket open.

That's when Finn saw the shoulder holster.

For an agonizing second, their eyes locked. Wells's face furrowed into an angry scowl of recognition. And the first thing he did was reach for his gun.

"Finn! Stop!" he called as he came toward them.

Gabi whispered, "This way!" and Finn had no choice but to follow her deeper into the woods. She pulled him along for a few yards and then pointed.

Directly in front of them stood an unassuming tree, like all the rest, only this one had two doorknobs screwed into either side of its trunk. They looked like two metallic mushrooms blooming from the bark. The metal was old and rubbed into a dull finish by the elements. Finn could see that the center of the ornately carved knobs had a keyhole. He momentarily panicked. Was he supposed to have a key?

"FINN!" Gabi screamed, looking over her shoulder at Wells.

And Gabi—Finn obviously couldn't leave Gabi behind now. Wells was lumbering over logs and underbrush close behind them and would catch up to them any moment.

The tree looked so ordinary. Nothing about it gave him the impression it would take them anywhere. He wondered if the doorknob would turn easily, or even at all. There were no instructions carved into the bark, nothing to tell him if they were supposed to hold on to one doorknob or two. It was all a wild guess.

Wells was barely an arm's length away now, with the weapon in his outstretched hand.

"With me!" Finn yelled to Gabi, his hand hovering over one doorknob. She nodded, placing her small hand over the second. "One, two, THREE!" They each grabbed hold and pulled.

Finn felt the cool wet metal against his palm and then a pulse of electricity. A blinding white light circled everything, formed a tunnel around reality. The last thing Finn saw was Gabi's eyes, wide and scared.

A loud noise muffled the sounds around him, including Wells's shouts.

Finn was wrenched forward and backward so hard he was afraid his neck would snap in two. He yelled for Gabi, only he no longer had a voice. He heard nothing but the roar of light—that's what it was. Light here had *sound*. It roared past his ears louder than any train or jet. The jolting was so rough on his body that the only thing he could do was go limp, so as not to fight it and cause himself more injury.

He was sure these were the final moments of his life. He shouldn't have even attempted to Travel. This wasn't for him. This was for Mom, Gran, and Faith. As these thoughts entered his mind, the roar and the pain increased. He needed to focus, to at least try to . . . to . . . steer?

Mom.

He silently called out to her. He imagined her

waiting for him. Smiling. Thrilled to see him. The air around him quieted and the buffeting lessened. He kept at it. She would be proud of him for finding the tree.

Only he hadn't, had he? It was Gabi who'd found it.

The buffeting increased. He tried to somehow push out the sounds. Tried to squeeze out the light.

Right when he was sure his body could take no more and he would be ripped in half, there came an abrupt silence. No more light, no more noise except for his ragged breathing. All around him was pitch black, and he had no idea where he was.

He could still feel the doorknob in his hand. Somehow he had never let go. He sank down against the tree. It was night and it was cold. Far too cold.

"Gabi? Are you okay?" There was no answer.

"Gabi!" He crawled around the tree on all fours, circling it. He was surprised to find his body obeying his brain's impulses. He'd been afraid every bone had been broken.

The ground was cold and wet. It was covered in snow!

"Gabi?" There was no answer. He was alone. "No! NO!"

The tree hadn't taken Gabi, which meant she was alone on the mountain with Wells and his gun.

Or worse—the tree could have taken her someplace different. He might never be able to find her again.

He couldn't bear to even think of the third possibility.

Finn began talking to himself in desperation. "If I hold on to the other doorknob again, maybe I can get back." He struggled to reach the other knob and whispered, "Hold on, Gabi, I'm coming."

A voice came out of the darkness and said, "It doesn't work that way."

CHAPTER 19

Finn couldn't trust his ears. It was too dark to see, but he could swear the voice was hers.

"I had to be sure it was you." He heard a sandpapery swish and the small explosive pop of a match being struck. The flame of an oil lamp sprang into existence. His eyes adjusted slowly.

"Mom?"

She was there in front of him, glowing in the weak amber light.

He staggered toward her, desperate to get a closer look. It *was* her. He fell into her arms, and she hugged him back tightly. She was real. Miraculously she was flesh and bone and real and *there*. Her arms were around him and he was crying and his nose was running like he was a snotty four-year-old all over again.

She cradled his head. "Oh Finn, I'm so sorry this has been hard on you. I'm so, so sorry."

Finn pulled away enough to look into her eyes. "What are you doing here? Why am I—"

"I've been hiding here. Oh, Finn. I knew you would find me."

"I didn't—I mean, it wasn't me. It was Gabi. She found the tree—and she—"

"Is she with you this time? Good. Don't worry, the tree would leave her behind."

"No! You don't understand. Mr. Wells is there with a gun!"

She frowned at this but reached out and squeezed his hand tightly. "I promise it will be okay. She'll be fine when you return. As for Mr. Wells, that will take a bit more explaining. I'm sure he's part of Doc Lovell's faction—"

"I knew it! Gran trusted him and then she didn't. She must have found out." He reached into his pants pocket and pulled out the list with Gran's warning.

Mom took it gently between her index finger and thumb, holding it up to the weak light of what Finn could now see was a brass lantern. She scanned the paper and then slowly folded it back up into a neat square. "This certainly confirms what I suspected all along, though she's never owned up to it in any timeline."

"Owned up to what?"

"That she misjudged him. That she was blinded with love. I think she figured it out too late." She handed him back the note with a solemnity that spoke volumes.

"You already know, don't you? You know that she's . . . dead?"

"Yes. I knew with me gone, she would Future Travel a lot in order to help us. She wouldn't be able to survive that many trips." She reached up and put her hand lovingly against his cheek. "You'll do anything for your child. I understand that now." Her voice cracked on the last words.

Finn could hardly believe she was real. He had done it. He had found Mom.

"Each trip forward in time took years off her life. She wasn't like me. I can go forward and see the results of my actions and then come back, without the deadly side effects. I can't keep returning to the same exact time over and over—if I do I get terribly sick when I return—but for your gran it was much worse."

Terribly sick. Her migraines. Gran's too.

He couldn't imagine Mom and Gran enduring what he just had, even once, much less repeatedly. Why would Gran do this when she knew it would kill her?

As soon as his mind formed the question he realized how dense he was being. It was for him. She was protecting him. Just like she tried to protect him from finding her body.

"And with all the closed nodes, it would be that much harder for her." Mom placed her hands on his shoulders and focused on his eyes as she spoke. It was hard to see in the dim light, but she looked thinner to Finn, and tired. "She loved you very much, Finn. We both do. It's what she wanted. She wouldn't have had it any other way. She was fully aware what crossing over closed nodes would do to her."

Finn swallowed and his throat hurt with the effort. He tried to focus on facts and data. "What do you mean? What's a closed node?"

"Nodes are very important to us. Traveling through time is a fragile thing. Imagine holding on to a long cord and going impossibly fast downhill. Nodes are like knots on that thread, they're where you can grab hold and then jump off. They're markers and landing points. There used to be many of them, all over the timeline. Now, someone's been locking them. The remaining open ones are years or even decades apart."

Finn took a breath to ask who was locking the nodes, but Mom's next words derailed his train of thought. "I chose to hide here because there are so many closed nodes in and around this moment in time. You found one of the few that's still accessible. When you Traveled here through the tree, it was painful, wasn't it?"

Finn wanted to point out what an understatement that was. "I thought I'd be torn apart."

"That's because it was your first time and there are so many closed nodes around this one. It will help to think of it like a thread next time, and hold on, feel for the nodes. When your mind comes across one, you can jump or hold on. Let yourself be guided by that thread and the trip won't be so violent."

Next time? There was nothing about that experience he wanted to repeat. "Why do I have to do it again?" His body shuddered at the thought.

"Because this is 1878."

"I'm in 1878?!" Finn looked around as if the year would somehow make itself evident. There was nothing but snow and trees. Then he realized Mom was using that brass lantern instead of a decent flashlight and wearing clothes that were certainly not ideal for the weather. A funny seed planted in his head: Was it possible time only made itself blatantly evident on humans and what they made?

As if in answer to his thoughts, Mom said, "This mountain has pretty much stayed the same for hundreds of years. The trails are fewer and more traveled, but otherwise you wouldn't be able to tell 1810 from 2010."

She reached slightly behind him and picked up what looked like a flannel blanket. She placed it around him and Finn was surprised at how heavy it was. It smelled like hay and horses. He wondered what kind of life she had made for herself here already. How long had it been for her?

"We've wanted to tell you for so long, your father and I. We told you too early before. This time, well, I think I have it all worked out correctly. I know what the last few weeks have been like for you." She paused and Finn could see her searching for the right words. "I'm sorry. It's not easy being a Traveler. It can be lonely. You have to keep secrets from those you love the most and sometimes you have to lie."

"You could have told me. I would have kept your secret. You didn't have to lie to me."

"It's not like that. I've always known I could trust you with anything. It's that my telling you at any given time has other consequences. A Traveler like me has to play out versions of history so many times with different choices, trying to choose the best possible one. It's hard to explain."

"Like chess. There are different ways the game can play out."

She looked surprised that he had already thought this through and gave him a faint smile. "Yes, I suppose it is a bit like chess. I've been trying to find the right choices, the right game I suppose, where you both suffer the least."

Finn thought about his dad. They *had* both been suffering. It was true. "Dad hasn't been at all like himself. He doesn't even talk to me anymore."

"Your father?" Mom seemed confused, as if she wasn't the one who had brought him up. "Oh James . . . I'm so sorry." She said this into the night as if his father would be able to hear it from more than one hundred years away. "Be kind to him, Finn. It's a hard life, being married to someone like me."

A loud snap of a twig came from their left. Finn

jumped up and was surprised at how ready he was to defend them both.

"Don't worry. We're safe here."

"Well, it's not safe back home!" Finn said. "Doc and Mr. Wells and the other members of ISTA are after me—and Gabi—"

Mom nodded. "Yes, I suspect Doc's trying to cover his tracks. He and some others in ISTA have been working against the majority. They believe the timeline should be altered, and they want to be the judges on how and what."

Finn blurted out the first thought that occurred to him. "Does Doc want to be the one to marry Gran?"

Mom gave him a surprised sort of smile. "Maybe, but I think ISTA's plans are more ambitious and far reaching than that. Doc and his faction of ISTA have been making decisions about what should be changed in history."

Finn's mind flashed to Gabi in the clearing, surrounded by sun and the bright green of the ferns. Where Finn had wasted no time in thinking of what he would change in his life, given the opportunity, Gabi was the one who thought of all it would change about their present. He wasn't sure he liked what that said about what faction of ISTA he would belong in. He wondered what their motivations to change the past were.

"I do not believe we should be the sole arbiters of what is best for the world," Mom went on. "Gran and her allies have always agreed with me. Doc went out on his own. I didn't see it right away, because a lot of the changed nodes were closed to hide the changes, but my imprints couldn't be erased."

"Imprints?" More language he didn't understand.

"Travelers can remember alternate timelines we've experienced. We call them imprints, because that's what they feel like, indelible stamps in the brain. Gran and her sisters have imprints too, but I'm the only one who has a *prime* imprint. I can see what the timeline originally looked like, before any Traveler altered it. As soon as Doc's allies began altering the timeline, I could sense the changes. Gran didn't believe it because her eyes were closed by her love for him."

"I don't get it. How could they fool you? You and Gran—you're the best."

She smiled faintly at him. "I see our reputation has reached you? Well, it's overstated. I can't Travel where nodes are shut. No one has ever been able to do that. We can Travel *over* them, but not directly to them. Once a node is shut, it can block an entire decade, sometimes more."

"But Doc can't time travel! How could he beat the two of you?"

"Oh, it's not only him. There are others who want to change the timeline, not protect it."

"Like Aunt Billie? But she's not very good! Aunt Ev told me."

"Did Aunt Ev help you this time? Good." A smile lived briefly on her face, then dissipated. "I've actually been wondering for a while if all Billie's bumbling is just an act. But it's far more serious than that. We're the only family of Travelers in Dorset, but there are more in other places."

So much for Aunt Ev's theory about Dorset marble being the source of the Travelers' power, Finn thought. Gabi would be disappointed.

"And the Others have a Traveler on their side more powerful than Gran and myself combined. A Traveler who can go back and forth in time without any limitations or side effects, and even shut the rest of us out of nodes."

"Who?"

"Your sister. Faith."

CHAPTER 20

It was as if Earth itself shifted on its axis.

"That's not possible. My sister's dead." He took ownership of her. *My sister.* He would prove his reality was not askew.

But even as he denied it, something inside his chest leapt to life. It was as if a long-dead piece of his charred insides sparked a flame.

"She's alive, Finn. She's always alive. They take her from us every time. That's why she was never found in the quarry." The sadness in her eyes was familiar even if this new story wasn't.

"But where is she? Who has her? Why didn't you go get her?" And then, the familiar anger. The feeling that he was only a pawn. "Why didn't you tell me? Do you have any idea what it's been like—what my whole life has been like—"

"I'm sorry." She rubbed tears away, and Finn noticed that the skin of her hands was calloused and cracked. "You have to understand that whenever I could tell you something, I have. I've been working to keep you both alive. Try and understand."

Both alive. Him and Faith.

Finn tried to imagine living hundreds of lifetimes inside only one. That's what Mom had been doing, and he never once had a clue. She was a computer playing the same game of chess over and over, only a computer had the benefit of not feeling any pain or being related to a sacrificed pawn. While Finn was growing up, she had always been there for him, always had time for him. In fact, she had all the time in the world. It must be exhausting. She did look tired and drawn, the light flickering over hollows in her cheeks that hadn't been there only a few weeks ago. How long had she been here?

Finn woke up his scientific brain. He began to assemble the known facts. "They took Faith because they knew . . . they knew what she'd be able to do."

"Yes. The latest daughter in the family line. The most powerful yet, with skills we could only guess at till she grew up. Someone they could use to bring about the utopia they envision. They think they're capable of making such decisions." She looked off into the distance and shook her head ever so slightly. "They send someone—sometimes it's Billie, sometimes it's one of the Others. In your timeline, they took her from us that day at the quarry."

Finn's mind was spinning. Many timelines existed in his world. It was true, and Gran and Mom could actually see them for themselves! "Why didn't you and Gran go back and change it? You can, can't you?"

"It happens over and over, Finn. If it's not the quarry, it's the lake, or the green, or the school. If it's not Doc himself, it's one or more of his allies. There is no stopping it. I've lived it over and over."

Finn had only lived it once and it was a crushing memory. He couldn't imagine how Mom dealt with so many memories.

"Someone always takes Faith and raises her—and tells her many lies. She is always turned against us, Finn."

Finn shuddered and shifted on the snow. It was melting through the horse blanket she had given him and his jeans were now wet. The cold didn't bother him as much as it should. There was a fiery ember inside of him now that kept repeating *She's alive.*

"You need to know something else about your

sister. Faith ends up doing terrible things. She grows into someone who can do great harm, without remorse."

"You're saying not only is Faith alive, she's also evil?"

"*Evil* is a finite word. Hearts can change, please remember that. It's a great emotional burden to do what we do. Faith developed her abilities at such a young age; it's too much knowledge for anyone, much less a child. Then the Others take her and influence her. I need more time with her, to help her understand her power."

Finn's brain flashed back to all the conversations that had abruptly stopped when he entered a room, the look in his parents' eyes when Faith's name was mentioned. For years Finn had been processing the information incorrectly, and it all had to be recalculated. The looks of disappointment weren't directed at him. They had been for Faith and what she had become.

He found himself hating everyone who was involved in her disappearance. Whoever took her had broken his family. Broken him.

The memories of that day came unbidden. First, the happy, calm ones. The look of his own chubby fingers playing in the shallows. The bright sun shining on the ripples of the water, glittering at him and making him wish they made a high tinkling noise.

There were disconnected snapshots of memory he could grab on to and hold in front of himself. The joy he'd felt in making his sister laugh. She had a loud little-girl belly laugh that was infectious. There was no way a little girl who laughed like that could grow up to be evil.

The good snapshots then quickly dissolved away into pain. The part where it all came crashing down. The frantic screaming of Faith's name by many grown-ups, him sitting alone on a rock crying and not knowing why. The word *lost* and all the dread it carried. Lost was the worst thing you could be at three years old.

And the worst memory: his father shaking his shoulders violently. "Did she go in the water? Did you see? Did you see *anyone else*?"

"My sister is alive and is an evil time traveler." Finn half-whispered this to himself in the hopes that it would become a logical statement upon utterance. It didn't. It sounded even more ridiculous out loud.

"I'm afraid it's worse than that, Finn," Mom said. "You have to go back there for me."

"Go where?"

She corrected him: “When.”

“I don’t understand.”

“I need you to go back to the day Faith was taken and bring her here, to me. You need to take her before they do.”

CHAPTER 21

"What? I can't do that!" Finn nearly fell backward in the snow at the suggestion.

"Yes, you can. You can use the tree. You got here, didn't you?" Something about the tone of her voice didn't ring true. It was the same tone she'd used when he was little and she was trying to cajole him into doing something.

Finn jumped up, crunched noisily through the snow back to the tree, and pointed to it.

"Why can't *you* go get her? And then we can all go home." Sure, it would be weird having to explain a sudden three-year-old sister who bore so much resemblance to Faith, but that's what the Firths did best. Weird.

Mom hadn't moved a muscle as Finn made his case. The way her coat fell around her made her look like she might be part stone. Rooted to the mountain.

"I can't, Finn. I have to stay here. I can't go back to that node again, not without risking my life. Repeated visits to the same node take a toll on me—similar to the effects that Future Travel have on Gran."

Finn flinched. "*Had* on Gran," he murmured. Mom looked away. "What about Dad? Could he use the tree?"

"No, it won't work for him. You have to be the one to do this, Finn. It's supposed to be you."

"Even if I can get back there, how am I supposed to grab Faith, get her all the way up the mountain, and bring her back to the tree? It took Gabi and me hours. How can I do that dragging a little kid?"

She looked at him funny for a moment, like she was sizing him up. She then stood up, revealing that her skirt was more voluminous than he'd thought—it went all the way past her ankles. She tugged at a cord around her waist and pulled something out of a small pocket that hung by a rope from her side.

"The portal will take you to the quarry this time. Put this on as soon as you have a good hold on Faith. It will bring you both back here."

Finn automatically reached for the object, out of curiosity more than acceptance of the task. He expected it to be another grounding stone. It was something entirely different.

He held it up in the meager light. It was a bright silver skeleton key that had been bent into a spiral shape. The loop of the warped shaft was the right size to fit around a finger. It was a ring. A "key ring," to be exact.

"It's all bent." It didn't look the least bit impressive.

"It's the key for the tree," said Mom. "You don't put it in the lock. You wear it. It will help you get back to the tree and then back to me. Show it to your father. He'll understand."

Everything in Finn's rational brain warred with what she was saying. Time travel could not possibly rely on such silly totems. It was about subatomic particles and quantum physics, not rocks and . . . and . . . jewelry!

"Why do I have to kidnap her? What if I just go back in time and warn Dad, and then he can keep us home that day, or—"

"No!" Her voice grew urgent. "They will keep taking her. They *do* keep taking her! You must understand, I've already tried the most obvious plans—I've played out so many options that you never even experienced. The only solution is to hide her somewhere else in time."

"Okay, even if I managed to bring her back," said Finn, fighting to keep the frustration out of his voice, "then what?"

"Then I keep her safe, here." She stretched out her arm and gestured to the darkness that surrounded them. Her wrist and forearm were thinner than before, like if she lost any more of herself she'd disappear entirely.

Suddenly Mom's plan became all too clear.

"You don't plan on coming home. You don't plan on coming back with me!"

Her face fell. Her eyes glistened in the glow of the lantern. He had figured her out.

"It's the only way, Finn. The only way that can work. We can make a difference. I can change what she becomes. She needs one of us to raise her, to love her, to teach her. It has to be me. Changing the future is not always easy, it's not always flipping a switch. Sometimes it takes . . . well . . . time."

Resentment exploded inside him. It created a vacuum and left no space for anything else. It was an anger he didn't know he was capable of until now.

"NO! I climbed the mountain to save *you*, not Faith! I need you home. Dad needs you at home. You don't get to choose her over us."

Finn couldn't stop the hot tears from rolling down his cheeks. They turned cold against his skin as they fell and he brushed them away with the back of his hand. Faith had always been more important.

"Oh, my darling boy. I'm not choosing her over you. I'm saving you. If this works, if I can change what she becomes, then I will be able to come home."

"So you've seen it. You've seen that this works?" He clutched the ring so hard it hurt.

She turned away and didn't answer him.

"You haven't, have you? You don't know for sure!" Finn paced through the snow. This was a horrible plan.

"No." Her tone was resigned. "I haven't seen it work like that . . . yet."

"Then no! I won't do it. You have to come back with me." Finn held the key out in his shaking hand.

She grabbed his hand, not the key, and held it still. Finn was astonished at how weak her grip was. Even when the migraines were at their worst, she had never seemed this fragile. He wanted to get her home, away from here. The 1800s had already not been kind to her. He toyed with the idea of dragging her to the tree. She was frail enough that he thought he might be able to. What he didn't know was if the tree would take them both if she resisted.

She was the one crying now, big tears streaming down her face and leaving wet trails of reflected light. "If you don't do this, if you let things go the way they are, she kills you, Finn. She kills you *and* me."

Finn dropped his arm and pulled away. He couldn't possibly be hearing her right.

"It's true. It's what she is now. She cares only about her own goals. She wants to control the timeline in entirety. She breaks away from the Doc and the Others. No one is able to control her. Don't you see? This is the only way. It's the only way you both survive."

His mind played a quick movie of a little girl running and laughing, images of a sweet curly-haired toddler framed around their house. These were the memories he had of Faith. She couldn't possibly have turned into someone who would kill her own family.

"Why? Why would she do that?"

"I wish I knew why people break, Finn. I don't have that answer. But I know you need to do this. You need to do it for me and your father, and also for Faith—and you absolutely need to succeed."

CHAPTER 22

Finn willed his frozen fingers to curve around the cold, hard metal of the doorknob. They hovered over it, refusing to clamp down. His body knew what was coming next and wanted no part of it. It was impossible to erase cellular memory.

"You can do it," Mom whispered. "This time remember what I told you about holding on to the thread. Think only about that day at the quarry. Focus. If you can find the strength to believe in it, without trying to reason it out, you can make it."

The hollows of her cheeks were still visible, and she seemed more than a little afraid for him. He wondered how dangerous this really was—and how much was she holding back to make sure he'd do it. How many lies would she be willing to tell to save him and Faith?

"What if I miss the node?"

"You won't. Keep thinking about that day. Remember the details. The node will grow larger as you concentrate and you won't miss it. Just make sure you concentrate on that day."

He reached into his pocket and felt for his meager arsenal. Gran's note, the grounding stone, and the skeleton key ring.

The light of the lantern flickered, making the knobs look as if they were jumping back and forth in the bark of the tree. For a moment he was afraid they were insubstantial things that would disappear if he didn't reach out at that second and grab hold.

"Now, Finn! You can do this." Mom's voice, cracking with the effort of the yell, stunned him into action.

He reached for both of the knobs this time and held on with all his might.

The white light took over, a stark contrast to the black of the night. He closed his eyes, but this was the kind of brightness that burned through eyelids. His knees buckled but he held on to the knobs, pressing his cheek hard against the tree and feeling the carving of the knobs dig into his palms. He imagined the palms of his hands being seared with a leaf garland tattoo. The feel of the bark against his face faded as the white blaze grew. He could no longer feel the ground below his knees. It was like being too close to a star, he thought, only there was no heat. It was just the light and its horrific sound, like the fabric of the universe being ripped in two. Finn desperately wanted to cover his ears, but he wouldn't dare try to take his hands off the knobs. He wasn't even sure if he could physically move in this space.

The vicious jolting began and Finn tried hard to find the thread Mom had mentioned. He couldn't see anything, he couldn't feel for it with his hands. He began to look for it in his mind like she'd said. He forced himself to look inside instead of outward, and what he found there was both frightening and breathtaking. There were many, many threads! They were everywhere in front of him, reaching out in all directions like millions of arteries and capillaries. He had no idea which one to grab on to. He began to panic and felt his heart beating hard within his chest as the roar of the light became more insistent.

No, Finn! he thought. *Go back inside yourself. Think about the day. Think about Faith.*

And as he thought about her laugh, her small hands and the color of her hair in the sun, one fiber out of the millions that lay before him began to glow and pulse. His mind soared closer to it and locked on. The roar became a muffled background thrum and he was no longer aware of any physical sensation. Gone was the feeling of his eyelids straining to keep out the light, or the pressure of his hands gripping the knobs of the tree. All that was left was the smoothness of the thread. More of a fiber—he reminded himself to mention this to Mom. It was smooth like silicone, if you could somehow feel silicone inside your brain. He slid effortlessly and quickly along it, thinking only of Faith's smiling face and belly laugh.

I'm coming to get you, Faith. I'm not going to let them have you.

CHAPTER 23

He felt occasional bumps, but they were small and inconsequential. A strong force continued to pull him toward his destination. He knew it was there, he could feel it like a gravitational pull. He gained speed as he went. Deep inside himself he also knew that the thread went on forever. He was still on the small piece that was his own lifetime, yet he sensed in his bones that beyond that, the thread would somehow feel different. That he could distinguish it. It was a strange kind of knowing, sitting at the base of his brain with no prior experience to explain it.

Finally the descent ended.

Finn could feel his body again. His eyes were still tightly shut against the bright light, only now, that light was warm. He was lying on his back in the grass, face up, his skin still cold from the mountain peak in winter, but quickly warming to the summer sun.

A cricket chirped close by and a bee buzzed past his nose. He pushed himself up on his elbows and opened his eyes. He was in a clearing in the woods—which woods he couldn't be sure. He hoped he was in the right place. His clothes were still cold from the snowy mountaintop, but the sun in the sky here was so hot that he could see steam coming off his wet jeans.

He stood up and got his bearings. He was on the mountain, right above the quarry. Up where the Fletchers lived. It didn't mean he'd found the right year, but at least he was correct geographically.

If he could do what Mom asked of him, he knew the chances of her returning with him were nonexistent. She would stay with Faith. It would take time to change the past, to change what Faith became. Only, how much time did Mom have? Thinking about the hollows in her cheeks made him shudder.

Deep down he also knew that she wasn't telling him the whole truth.

Suddenly he heard the unmistakable high-pitched squealing of children playing. He got up and moved closer to the tree line.

He knew those voices. He knew that laugh. It

tugged at him through the years like a lasso around his heart. He followed it without thinking, peering through the bushes.

There was the quarry. He was deep in the brush on the highest point of the cliff, the narrow edge of the rectangle farthest from the road. Three figures—two children and a man—perched far below him on the lowest ledge of marble blocks. He couldn't distinguish features from this far away, but he didn't need to.

He found the dirt path that wound around the cliff, and followed the voices down toward the water. He emerged from a new vantage point, much closer.

He saw himself first. A toddler. It felt like he was in the wrong place. As if his consciousness had been thrust out and shoved onto the bank of the quarry. It was a bit like an out of body experience, yet the little boy's body was completely foreign. It seemed impossible that he had ever been that small. The surface of the greenish water was sparkling in the sun, just as he remembered it, and Finn watched in fascination as his younger self dipped his hand into a plastic bucket full of the water, held his dripping wet hand up, and studied the way the sun glinted off the droplets. He recalled the memory from the other side, holding up his small hand and feeling complete joy in discovering something new about the way water and light worked together. This was the happy memory that had stuck with him, the memory before it all went bad.

Finn forced himself to blink.

Faith laughed and inched closer to young Finn. She sat sitting cross-legged on the marble slab with him. It was Faith, right there in front of him. She was there in entirety. That was what surprised Finn the most. He could see all of her, whereas in his memories she was always made up of fragmented snapshots: a closeup of her fingers, smiling eyes, a small mouth laughing at him. He was never far enough away from her to get the full picture.

Now, here she was in front of him to see all at once. He was an exile on the banks, watching the joy from afar. He wanted so badly to be closer. He had the sudden urge to pick her up and hug her and tell her he loved her. Tell her that all the years without her had felt so wrong. That twins aren't meant to be separated. He felt like the protective older brother now, even though they were the same age.

He was transfixed by both of them. It was like a movie he couldn't tear his eyes away from. Where tiny Finn was quiet and contemplative, tiny Faith was loud and joyous. Her giggle rose up over everything else, and her small arms continued to toss water in the air as high as she could get it to go. Finn watched his younger self cup both hands and dip them down into the bucket, then bring the little well of water up over his head and let it dribble into his hair.

Faith exploded into giggles again.

He had remembered her laugh perfectly. The little memory flashes he carried with him floated in and out of his subconscious. Sometimes it was a round face smiling conspiratorially, waiting for him to do the next thing to make her laugh. Nearly all of his memories were of her smiling or laughing, and now as he watched the scene below it became clear why. He was the one responsible for putting that smile there. Now he remembered. She had been his audience and he was her clown. This was as surprising to Finn as if someone had told him the earth was flat—and just as incongruous. He had no clue how to make anyone laugh now.

They had been a team. She had to be good—no—she *was* good. Finn began to feel ashamed at himself for second-guessing Mom. She was right. He had to save her, save her from Doc and Aunt Billie and whomever else was involved.

He tried not to think about what it would mean for *his* life. It didn't matter right now.

Faith's squeals of delight brought Finn back to the urgency of this moment. He looked around to see if he was alone in spying. Miraculously, no one else was nearby. He had forgotten how quiet the quarry could be when he was little, before the internet found it and tourists started flocking in.

Behind the twins, an impossibly young, slimmer version of Dad leaned against one of the marble slabs, absent-mindedly smiling at both children. Dad had that same detached look Finn knew so well, as if he were focused on something far away. No, not detached. Finn could see something else in his face now. He was on guard. Vigilant. Protecting them.

That concentration, the constant preoccupation, it was fear. His father's eyes were studying the scene. Scanning the tree line, scanning the water. All those times when he was so preoccupied with work began to make sense. He studied history to protect his family. This was his father's real job. Part of Finn wanted to run over and hug him and apologize for every mean thing he'd ever said—for every time he'd thought that Dad was letting him down.

A deep sadness began to grow inside him as he

realized what his father's future looked like. Even if it was for the best, it was now Finn's own actions that would break his family apart.

He was going to take Faith away.

CHAPTER 24

Finn tried to imagine how to approach the happy scene. He could walk right up and talk to Dad. Would Dad even recognize him? He hoped Mom had explained at least some of what would happen.

Taking a deep breath, Finn left the path and cut through the trees. It was a noisy descent, but he figured it was better than sneaking up on them.

Dad saw him right away. His hand went to his side—a reflex, the kind of thing people did when they were armed. Finn froze and put his hands out where his father could see them. He had never known his dad to carry a weapon of any kind, ever.

Their eyes met and Dad's hand relaxed. They stood ten feet apart now, staring at each other. Seconds that felt like an eternity. It wasn't that Dad actually looked that much younger—he looked very much the same, only less beaten down.

"You don't look anything like I expected," Dad said. He stepped closer and Finn fought the urge to step backwards. His father's scrutinizing stare was too focused, too intense. "You look like your mother's family. You're tall."

Finn could only nod. He had no idea what to say.

The children noticed him now and came toward him with curious looks on their faces. It hurt to look his younger self in the eye. A physical pain shot through his head, like he was chewing on tin foil. He focused on Dad instead.

"So it worked then," Dad said. "You were able to get to her?"

"Yes. It wasn't easy." Finn wished he could explain that first trip, but the words failed him. Dad looked away from him back toward the children. Faith and young Finn were doing that thing that children do when a stranger appears. They were cautiously standing behind their father, peering at big Finn like he was some kind of exhibit at the museum.

"I'm supposed to—"

Dad cut him off. "I know the plan, and I'm afraid I'm not on board. I've always trusted your mother about these things, but this seems too extreme, even for her."

Finn figured his dad had the same misgivings he did, but he couldn't let on that he felt them too. This wasn't the time to have a philosophical discussion.

"She told me I had to hurry. I'm sorry, but I think she's right. I think I'm here for exactly this reason. I realize now, for as long as I can remember I've felt angry and guilty about—what happens today." He nodded his head ever so slightly in Faith's direction. He couldn't say anything more specific in front of them, even if the children wouldn't yet understand. "I was wrong, Dad. I think it has to happen, and it was supposed to be me all along."

Dad's eyebrows rose in shock. It occurred to Finn that this was the first time anyone had called him Dad. The Finn behind his pant leg right now would still be calling him Daddy. Maybe that was what shook him.

"She told me to show you this." He held the ring out in his upturned palm. Faith went up on her tiptoes to get a better view of what he was holding. Young Finn stayed hidden behind his father.

Dad reached out for the ring and took it from Finn's hand before he had a chance to protest. He turned it back and forth between his fingers studying it.

"She gave you *this*?" It was a question tinged with incredulity. It annoyed Finn. Why wouldn't she give him something as important as the key to the portal?

"Yes, and I need it if we're going to get back."

Young Finn stepped forward now, his eyes boring into big Finn's brain. Finn focused on the boy's small protruding belly instead. *His* belly, round and childlike. New memories flooded his field of vision and he did his best to push them aside.

"Hello, Finn. Hello, Faith. I'm a friend of your mother."

He instantly wished he hadn't addressed his younger self. The memory was almost too much to experience alongside the present reality. It was easier not to talk to him. Whatever he said echoed back in his own mind, a long-ago fuzzy impression. It was beyond disorienting.

Finn could sense Dad tensing up next to him. Still, he crouched down and looked Faith in the eyes. He wasn't very good at talking to little kids. Gabi was the one who was good at that, the way she got the younger kids at the theater camp to follow her around like the pied piper while her mother manned the phone. Finn tried his best to channel Gabi and looked Faith right in the eyes. At least her memories wouldn't instantly be implanted in his brain.

"Do you think we can be friends?"

The child shook her head slightly and hid further behind her father's legs. She couldn't possibly know what he was there for or what it would mean for her life, but she was afraid of him anyway. Smart girl. Finn wondered what kind of enemy she could grow to be.

"Listen . . . Finn." His father stumbled over the name. Finn's younger self looked up at Dad questioningly. "I think she's missing something, some vital piece of the puzzle. There has to be another way. I won't let her go."

At that, Faith looked at her father and stepped back. A frightening understanding was growing on her face. She was only a toddler, but she knew the word "go" and she didn't know this big tall boy in front of her. She began to cry. A quiver of the lip first, and then she grabbed fistfuls of her father's pants and sobbed.

"Faith, calm down." Dad knelt beside her. "It's okay. Daddy's not going anywhere." It wasn't exactly a lie, Finn thought. Daddy wasn't.

Dad looked back at Finn. "You can see it, can't you? It'll be far too traumatic. It's an unnecessary plan for a disaster that may not even happen."

"It happens. Today." Finn looked away toward the water. Unbidden images of a child floating in green water came to his mind, but that wasn't right anymore. *What happens is someone takes her. They'll tell young Finn it was a drowning.*

Why didn't Dad know all this? "Didn't she tell you?"

It was Dad's turn to look away. "Sometimes she doesn't tell me things. We both agreed it's better that way." His eyes widened. "This must be why she stayed home today. She couldn't stomach this."

"But she's relying on us." Finn began to look around nervously. He had no idea who would be coming for Faith, but he wanted to be long gone before they arrived.

"Who? Who does it?" Dad's question was insistent and angry.

Finn realized he was without the details necessary to sway his father. "I don't know who specifically . . . but it's Doc you can't trust."

Dad's mouth twisted up at one corner. Finn didn't know if he was absorbing this information or formulating a plan to get the children away from him. His next question came out of the blue.

"Did she look okay?"

"Mom?" The tenderness of the question made Finn swallow hard before answering. He remembered her thin wrists and hollowed out cheeks. He thought about lying, but it didn't seem right. "No. She looks too thin."

They studied each other for a moment and Finn wanted to tell him everything. How Mom had no intention of coming home. How this was good-bye to Faith and in a few years it was good-bye to Mom, too. Unless—unless she could somehow beat the odds. Because that was what altering time was, a gamble. Nothing was sure. He realized it now. It was all playing the odds, and in Mom's case she was playing them over and over again.

Dad spoke before Finn could. He was resolute. "You can have the ring back, but that's all you're taking with you. I can protect my family."

He pushed the ring into Finn's palm and held on tighter to Faith's hand. Her little fingers were completely wrapped in his fist.

"But Dad, it's today!"

"I don't care. I don't want to know what's next. I trust that I can protect my family. That's what I'm asking of you. Man to man."

His last three words were a shock to Finn. The Dad he knew in his time would never give him that label. He was dealing with Finn like an equal. It filled Finn with momentary pride.

They were interrupted by the sounds of leaves rustling on the trail behind them. Finn shot Dad a look of horror. This was it. They were here.

"Run," Dad hissed. "Don't let anyone see you!" He pushed Finn backward behind one of the giant marble slabs.

Finn, realizing he could still be seen from the trail, sprinted for the other path that led to the opposite side of the cliffs. He tried to be as soundless as possible.

His mind raced as he tried to decide what to do next. He could go back to Mom now. Tell her he'd failed. Insist she come home—home to the present—with him.

She'd never forgive him. He'd never forgive himself.

He circled the quarry and stopped above the highest cliff, the ones Sebastian and his friends had just been jumping from only yesterday. *No*, he corrected himself. *They haven't jumped here yet.* He was years before them.

He was directly across from Dad and the twins now, only thirty yards of water separating them. He could hear their voices echo off the steep marble walls and across the water.

"James . . ."

Doc.

Finn leaned through the branches, desperately trying to see and hear what was happening.

Doc was not alone. There were three other men with him. That was both bad and good. The three men were large and imposing, but no women meant no one could take Faith directly from this node into another time; they'd need to bring her to someone who could Travel. Finn looked around, scanning the tree line, and his heart dropped when he found what he was looking for. Down in the parking lot, leaning against Doc's ancient Jeep, was the unmistakable skeletal silhouette of Aunt Billie. She was waiting, with paper-thin arms folded, waiting to destroy Finn's world.

Dad, holding Faith in his arms, stood facing the men. "Yes, Will. I know." He was speaking loudly. He wanted Finn to hear. "*It is the greatest happiness of the greatest number that is the measure of right and wrong.* I've heard it all before."

Finn could see Doc's mouth moving, answering, but the words were lost across the water.

"We might be more inclined to trust ISTA if you stopped holding meetings behind our backs," Dad said.

Doc's angry voice echoed across the marble stones. "You've given us no choice. You've behaved irrationally. And James, we do understand. We can't blame you. It's an impossible decision." He turned to one of the men behind him and nodded. "One we feel we must make for you."

Two of the men were suddenly on top of Dad. He yelled "No!" and held Faith tightly. Finn could no longer hear, and he couldn't see their faces from this far, but he could suddenly remember them. The horror of the moment was being built in his three-year-old brain to echo in his older self's memory. He was witnessing it from two angles. The men held Dad back as he fought hard against them, and one of them wrenched Faith from Dad's hands.

The third man picked her up with no effort. She was so small against his hulking form. He had one arm around her middle and the other around her neck. Young Finn was crying and shaking, frozen in fear.

The large man yelled out in pain. Faith bit him!

He dropped her, cradling his forearm. Faith bolted. She sped up the trail on her tiny legs, the same way Finn had just come.

Doc and the injured man chased after her. The large, hulking man was cradling his arm against his side and Finn could see blood trickling through his clenched fingers.

"Good girl," Finn whispered. "You got him."

She was running the same path Finn had just taken, the path that encircled the whole quarry. As long as she continued on the trail that skirted the quarry's edge, she'd be heading straight for him. He would be ready. He'd grab her and put on the ring and get her to Mom. Dad would understand. There were no other options.

But Faith was moving fast and with the gracelessness of a child consumed by fear. Finn held his breath as she skirted the far end—and stumbled. Her small wet feet skidded across the rock, her tiny arms reached for the empty air around her as she slid sideways off the marble cliff, plunging awkwardly to the deep water below.

"No!" Finn screamed and swore. He heard his father do the same from the opposite shore. Finn had the worst view—watching helplessly from two perspectives, in his memories of his three-year-old self and in the moment now.

Poised on the edge of the highest cliff, he didn't even have to think. The memory and the inclination came at once.

He dove headfirst into the quarry.

CHAPTER 25

The water was clearer than Finn expected—he could make out the walls of the marble on either side, but the depths below him were pure black. He surfaced and took a gulp of air and dove under again, as deep as he could. There ahead of him was a small black sliver of a child, desperately trying to kick herself up toward the light.

He reached forward into the blackness, and a tiny hand grabbed him with all its might.

He pulled hard, doing his best to get them up to the surface for air. But she felt impossibly heavy, immovable. He looked down and realized her foot was stuck. Wedged between rocks. She was holding on to Finn for dear life. He tried to wrench her free to no avail. He was running out of time—

And then he realized there was only one way out.

He reached into his pocket and grabbed the ring.

At that same moment, Faith tried to use him to pull herself free, yanking hard down on his arm. The ring tumbled out of his hand.

NO!

It sank miraculously slowly, floating and glinting in the little light that the depths of the quarry let in. Finn kicked forward enough to grab it and held on to Faith as tightly as he could with his other arm. He clenched his hand into a fist to protect it. It would have to be enough.

The roaring light came as Finn pulled Faith close in a fierce bear hug. He felt her body go limp and stop struggling, and he hoped with every fiber of his being she was still alive. The entire bottom of the quarry lit up in a blaze of bright white, and then it was gone.

The jolting back and forth began. Finn braced himself and searched his subconscious for the thread, the anchor to hold on to. Whatever happened, he wasn't letting go of Faith.

Faith was definitely there. He couldn't see her or feel her anymore, only sense her presence, small but powerful. She was alive.

Are you okay? He tried to speak to her but

remembered speaking here was impossible. He thought it instead. *Are you all right, Faith?*

She didn't answer, but he felt her resigned acquiescence, mixed with overwhelming fear.

Look for Mommy, Faith. Think about Mommy. The term felt strange to him, though he knew it would be the one Faith used for their mother. And it worked—he could sense that the thought of Mom soothed her.

This trip already felt easier than the last two. Calm, almost hypnotic. Finn instantly realized why. It was Faith. She must be the one driving. Of course! She didn't need a ring or a tree. She could Travel on her own. She must be taking him along for the ride.

Finn wrapped his mind around the timeline with her and together they slid along it, looking for the pulsing, glowing node that was the right one. It was a slower, more manageable acceleration this time. Finn almost felt like they had time to feel each node before they reached it. The noise of the white light wasn't nearly as loud either. The whole thing was less disorienting. He wondered if this was even the first time Faith had Traveled.

You're doing great, Faith. Just look for Mommy. She's waiting for us.

She didn't answer him. When he reached out

toward her in the space of blinding white, all he felt was her fear and confusion. It probably *was* her first time. He would have to help her find the right node.

Suddenly, he felt the tremble on the thread. It was small and far away, like the tremor of a spider's web touched by a falling leaf. Then it became more prominent. Finn could feel it before he could see. This was it.

It's coming, Faith. This is where we need to go.

She began to resist the descent. He felt her pulling away from it and from him. *No! This is where we're supposed to be, Faith. Mommy is there.* He tried to guide her toward the node and off the thread, but she pulled away from him in a fierce panic.

Faith, listen. It's Finn. I'm Finn. All grown up and I'm telling you it's going to be okay. Mommy is going to be here. I'm bringing you to Mommy.

She began to calm. The pulling away was less intense.

She's going to hug you and she's going to tell you everything is going to be okay and she's going to take care of you . . .

It came to him completely unbidden: the selfish thought. It was for just a split second. A flash of resentment was all it was. She was going to get

Mom. Faith, after everything she'd done, or would do, she was going to have Mom and he'd still be left alone. It was only a fleeting emotion, but here in the threads of time it was magnified. It telegraphed out of him in every direction and he could feel the truth of it hit her.

He could feel the questioning panic coming from young Faith now. In this timeless space he could sense her emotions and she could sense his.

She was terrified of him.

She was only a little kid. He knew this. He had let that horrible resentment take hold of him. In that split second of anger, he thought of her as someone who would grow up with the capacity to murder him. He tried hard not to think about what she would become, but the thing about trying hard not to think about something is that it makes you think about it all the more.

Her fear became something he could almost touch. It pulsed all around him, and he panicked as he felt her begin to recede from him. She was no longer next to him. She had let go of the thread. She was receding in the white light. He desperately tried to reach for her in this space where no part of him could do the reaching.

He knew what that felt like, how horrible it was

to be buffeted around in this plane of existence. It felt like you were on a saucer endlessly tipping in all directions and you couldn't reach any one side to hold on to before it tipped again.

Faith! Come back! I'm sorry. I'm sorry!

He pushed the words out to her. Nothing came back. He tried to pull her back in, but she was moving ever farther away. Farther away from him and the node he was sure was the right one. The one where Mom would be waiting.

Faith. Please. I'm sorry. Please come to me. Let me take you to Mommy.

Faith was still moving away and the only thing he could do was to let go and follow her, leaving the node where Mom was waiting far behind.

CHAPTER 26

Faith whimpered next to him, and he slowly became aware of his arms. He was holding her tight against his wet chest and she wasn't struggling anymore.

"It's okay, Faith. It's okay," he lied as he sat up.

He could feel Faith's tiny arms trembling in the cold already. He had taken her from a hot summer day, where she'd been soaking wet and near drowning, to the depths of winter. They were both soaked to the bone. He had no idea when they were. The air tasted like snow and it was bitterly cold. Could they have been that lucky? Did Faith actually bring him to the top of the mountain where Mom was waiting?

"Hello, Finn."

A strong beam of light blinded him in the darkness.

"Let her go," a woman's voice ordered from the other side of the light.

Finn shielded his eyes with his forearm. "Mom?"

There was a mocking laugh. "I suppose it makes sense that we'd sound alike. Try again."

The flashlight moved, thrown to the ground. Finn could just begin to see the outline of a young woman moving between trees. She was holding another woman around the neck.

Mom.

As his eyes became accustomed to the darkness he could also see something bright and silver in the other woman's hands, pressed against Mom's neck.

"Thanks for doing all the hard work for me, brother."

Faith. A grown-up Faith was standing in front of him. She wore a long gray coat buttoned up to her chin. Her cheeks were red with the cold, and her hair and eyes were the same colors Finn saw in the mirror each morning. The family resemblance was uncanny. She looked like a younger version of Mom and at the same time she was undeniably his twin.

She pushed Mom over to a tree stump and forced her to sit down, still keeping the knife at her throat. This was a different Mom, a Mom even more malnourished than before. She was wearing layers of old-fashioned clothing and a knit scarf. She was bony, all angles. Finn was sure she could be broken in half.

Frantically, he took in the surroundings, very different than the mountaintop he knew. A clearing had been made, with a dilapidated shed off to the right and the woods surrounding them. The snow was deep around his legs, and his body was starting to shake violently—or was that young Faith? He held her more tightly to his chest, trying to give her all his warmth, while searching Mom's eyes for some consolation, but her eyes only mirrored his defeat.

"Faith, come sit by your mommy. It's okay. I won't hurt *you*." The woman was speaking to her younger self with a syrupy kindness that made the girl shrink farther into Finn's arms.

"It's okay, baby. It's me," Mom pleaded.

Young Faith let go of Finn cautiously. His instinct was to pull her back, but the child moved toward her mother like a magnet and he didn't stop her.

As Finn stood up, though, she turned back, shaking violently in the cold, and took one last questioning look at him. There was something new in her face besides fear. Finn began to wonder if the little girl was finally ready to trust him. He held out his hand to her and willed her to know that he was sorry.

"Careful, Finn. If you so much as touch her, I will slice our mother's throat wide open. I'd be doing her a mercy. Her future is bleak from here on out."

"Please, Finn. Do as she says." Mom's voice was shaky. Finn couldn't tell if it was from the cold or fear.

Young Faith was now taking in the situation and she slid one step backward, toward Finn. She watched the woman with the knife carefully. Adult Faith was imposing and tall. The child was confused—she had no way of knowing she was staring at her future self. Finn wondered if adult Faith had the same dizzying sense of memories being created in her head that he'd experienced at the quarry. If so, it didn't seem to affect her at all. Her face was calm and full of purpose, though Finn could swear she was trembling with rage, not cold.

"Child, if you don't listen to me right now you won't have a mother at all."

"Go, Faith, it's okay. Sit by Mommy."

It was Finn who she finally obeyed. She ran to Mom, collapsing in the billows of her skirt and coat. Without moving her head, Mom splayed five fingers over her hair and quietly promised her it would all be okay. She opened her coat and let Faith curl up inside next to her. All this she did calmly with the blade still poised at her throat.

Adult Faith drew in a breath and smiled. She pulled the knife away from Mom's neck and Finn's knees nearly buckled with relief.

"You saved me an awful lot of trouble, Finn. I should thank you . . . but I won't." They were at the edge of the clearing, and behind him Finn could almost hear the trees cracking and groaning with the weight of snow and ice. The shed was so tiny that even labeling it a shed was generous. They obviously hadn't come back on the same night he left. How long had Mom waited for them?

Adult Faith spoke to him again. "Now that the child is in my care, none of you can change a thing. It's over. I win."

"What could possibly be the purpose of kidnapping yourself?" Finn demanded.

"Little Faith here needs the proper training. Don't you, darling?" The hand without the knife leaned over to brush against the child's head, but young Faith sank farther away and Mom shifted her body to shield her. Adult Faith's mouth twisted in anger, and she quickly regained composure.

"She doesn't know it yet, but the entire universe is hers for the taking. Once we get rid of certain obstacles, of course." She flicked the wrist holding the knife and gestured toward Mom.

Finn jumped forward.

"No, Finn! Don't!" Mom cried.

Faith laughed. "Go ahead, Finn. Come at me." She threw the knife far away into the field of snow. "Look, I'm defenseless."

Finn stayed still. He knew enough bullies to recognize a trap. He needed to keep her talking—needed more data before he chose his next move.

"Smarter than you look." She turned her back toward him as if he was unimportant, gesturing over her shoulder as she spoke. "The knife was just for show, you know. I don't need a weapon." She walked a few more feet away from him and then, WOOSH, she was in his face so quickly he flinched. "I *am* the weapon. I am the last in the family line. I have all the powers of our mother here, times ten."

"You can't create a portal," Mom chimed in. She was standing now, with young Faith behind her, wrapped in her coat.

Faith whirled around and stomped toward Mom, as young Faith disappeared completely behind Mom's skirts. She raised one long elegant finger up to Mom's face. "You have one little trick you've figured out before me. That's all. And when I'm through here, you'll show me how you did it."

"I won't." Mom's voice was calm and resolute.

"Oh, but I'm banking on you being such a great mother . . ." Faith's voice was cloying and full of venom. "Surely you'll want to teach little Faith here all your tricks. You do plan on being a good mother, don't you? You want her to grow up to be a good and decent girl." She laughed.

Finn shook with rage. He couldn't help himself. Regardless of what she could do to him, he was going to fight.

He stepped forward. "L-l-leave them alone!" His voice quaking as he shook with the cold.

She turned back to Finn and smiled. "You want me to leave them alone? Give me the ring."

"No."

"Finn," his mother called to him. "It's okay. Please. Give it to her."

It was against everything in Finn's makeup to believe in a magic key ring, but that was exactly what it had become for him. He didn't want to hand it over, but when he studied Mom's face he saw a certainty there that couldn't be ignored. She was staring at him with laser focus. There was no fear in her eyes. She wanted him to do it.

He took off the ring and tossed it on the ground in front of him. It sank into the untouched snow.

Faith strode forward and fished it out, held it up like it was a symbol of victory. She smiled wide.

"Do you know what you are, brother? You're a footnote." In an instant she had moved forward so that they were face to face again. It was a menacing trick that worked just as well the second time. Her breath was hot in the icy air and smelled of licorice. She leaned in and whispered, "You are nothing but a useless collection of blood and guts. You are the leftover genetic material of *me*."

He winced at the description. It was how he'd always felt.

She laughed. "Don't you get it? I'm always smarter than you. I'm always three steps ahead of you. Technology you haven't even dreamed of yet is at my disposal. I'm always going to win."

"You're wrong," Mom said, still standing firmly in front of young Faith. "You need him. He's your brother."

Faith whirled toward her again. "Oh, are we

going to talk about family honor? Please. You're the worst of all! How many times have you abandoned me, let me go? I've seen it all, in countless timelines. I've seen how you've lived on without me. How little you've done to find me. You! Who could have done anything."

"Faith, everything we've done—"

"You've done for *me*, right? Don't lie to me, Mother. You sent me away. You gave me away to strangers! Do you even know what happened in that timeline? Do you? It doesn't matter. I saved myself. I found some Dorset marble. It's everywhere, up and down the eastern seaboard, allowing me to Travel. I bested you even without knowing who I was or where I came from."

Mom's voice faltered. "I don't know—I never did that."

"Oh, but you did, just not in this universe. I can see them all. Each and every timeline in each and every universe. I know you better than anyone. Do you know what your deepest sin is? The one that tops even abandoning your child? You have consistently sat by politely and watched the world go on its horrific way without using your power to change it. You stand by and do nothing while cities burn! I am not afraid to use my gift."

"And what have you accomplished, Faith? What have you changed?"

Faith laughed. "I've only just started. I can close nodes to the rest of you—and still access them for myself. Soon I'll have whole sections of the timeline sealed off for my own use. This timeline and all its neighbors will be mine alone to shape."

She was busy arguing with Mom—Finn could rush her now. Tackle her to the ground and . . . and what? He had never been in a real fight in his life. In truth, he was petrified. She could come back and change any course of action he took. He couldn't change the future or the past.

And then the memory came to him, the snippet of the dream. He saw himself being surrounded by swelling stars. Stars like the twinkling sunlight in drops of water. Mom's voice from the past: *People are who they are. All you can control is how you treat them.* The shiny iridescent stars that keep growing and swelling ever larger, that was the best you could leave behind.

He looked at both Faiths. One was beyond reaching and the other would likely never remember today. His chances weren't good.

He studied young Faith, and he saw innocence and fear. If this woman in front of him wouldn't listen, maybe the child would.

He bent down low and called to her. "Faith . . ."

Both Faiths trained their eyes on him. He spoke only to the child.

"I'm sorry. We're here because of me. Because of what I thought on the thread. It's not your fault. I'm always going to love you, Faith. You're my sister and I'm always going to love you. Do you understand?"

The little girl still stayed close to her mother, clutching Mom's overcoat. Finn refused to look away until she acknowledged him in some way. She was trembling with both fear and cold, but she looked directly into Finn's eyes and nodded nearly imperceptibly. He felt the understanding. Something inside Finn cracked and opened, made his chest explode in warmth and rippled through him all the way to his fingers.

It was similar to how he'd felt at the quarry, but bigger, more far-reaching. It was as if this moment synched up with countless others, as if it were the missing piece of an impossibly long equation. For a split second Finn felt as if he were an old man, and a teenager, and a little kid, and someone his dad's age, and all the versions of him were saying the same thing—all sharing the same feeling, radiating the same truth.

Finn forced himself to turn away and see how Faith's older self was handling the instant memory build. Finn watched as her mouth contorted and her eyes squinted with confusion. For a moment, Finn began to think that time didn't matter at all. What mattered was memory. If he could change Faith's memories, make this one stick with her, maybe this was the key.

Adult Faith focused back on him, suddenly full of fury and hatred. She held up both hands and screamed, "NO!"

Her gesture was so familiar to him, like he had experienced it from the other side at some point. The church. Aunt Billie.

Finn heard his mother scream in horror, "Faith, no! Please!" and then he heard nothing more.

CHAPTER 27

The pain was so bad Finn wanted to sink back into unconsciousness. Faith had pushed him out of the node. He was Traveling, but he was nowhere near the thread. It felt like a thousand sharp knives were being plunged into his brain as he was hurtling through nothingness. He knew he was screaming past nodes at an impossible speed. He couldn't even try to fight it if he wanted to. His mind was incapable of doing anything but managing the searing pain inside his head.

He desperately searched for a thread. There was nothing near him, or maybe he was just going too fast. Faith had thrown him off the node, cast him outside the timeline with no anchor. He had no idea where he was going or if he'd ever land. This could be his eternity.

He remembered Aunt Ev's stone in his pocket, only how could he grab it when he had no control over his body? Just trying to think about something as normal as moving his hands made the pain intensify. The blades in his head dug deeper and made it impossible to think. The realization came to him all at once: He wouldn't survive this for long. No human being could.

With his last remnant of consciousness, he called out to Mom, Dad and then . . . Gabi.

With the thought of Gabi, the blades inside his head started to slow their attack.

Gabi. Gabi. Gabi.

He held on to the name like a beacon. *Just get me back to Gabi.*

He felt a brilliant burst of amber light. The color was gentle, like the sun through a filter of yellow and orange tree leaves on an autumn day. It appeared like an orb in front of him. He reached for it.

ooo

"He showed up here looking like this. He looks absolutely terrible. Is he okay?"

"He'll be all right. Thank you, Sophia. I don't

know what we'd do if you hadn't recognized him."

"I still don't quite understand it all."

"I know. I'll explain more in time. For now, can you promise to keep this secret for me? I know it's a lot to ask. But he'll be in terrible danger if you tell anyone."

"Of course. I've kept them all, Liz. I won't stop now."

A warm, soft hand was caressing his forehead.

"Mom?" He forced open dry, crusty eyelids and found himself in Gabi's living room.

Mom and Mrs. Rand were there. The fireplace was lit, but no other lights shone in the small space. He tried to pull himself up on his elbows but couldn't find the strength. He felt like the husk of a human, dried-out and hollow. The confusion that surrounded him began to lift.

"Mom! You're okay!" He croaked this out. The relief was almost too much for him to take. He was waking from a days-long bad dream. That must be it. He was still trying to find his voice. "I thought I was dying. I didn't think I'd ever get back."

"It's okay, Finn. I'm going to take you back home now."

"Where's Faith? Where's Gabi? Are they okay?"

There was an awkward pause and then Mom answered, "Gabi is upstairs sleeping in her bed. Don't worry."

"How did she get off the mountain?"

Mrs. Rand shot his mother a look of fear. "Were you on the mountain together, Finn?"

"Yes! We found the tree, just like Gran said. I brought Faith to you and the tree—it didn't take Gabi!"

Mom grabbed Finn's hand tightly and turned to Mrs. Rand. "I just had the idea. The fact that he's here tells me it's a good one. I haven't even fully hashed it out yet. Gabi is safe upstairs. I promise."

Finn was surprised at the obvious closeness between his mother and Mrs. Rand. This was something he had never witnessed before. They'd always been acquaintances at most.

Mom returned her attention to Finn. "Gabi is upstairs asleep, Finn. It's the year Gabi moved in. You somehow found yourself here and that's good. You made it. I can take you the rest of the way home. What year did you come from, Finn?"

If this was back in third grade, that could only mean that back in his time everything was as messed up as he left it. The crevice in his chest began to open, threatening to swallow him whole once more. That moment of elation had been too cruel. He looked at Mrs. Rand and could see that her hair was shaggier, longer. The way it was when he first met Gabi.

"When did you come from?" Mom asked again.

Home had never been a year coordinate before. It had always been a street address. In this new life he realized he now had two addresses. He had a hard time focusing. "It's September . . . before my thirteenth birthday. Mom, things are bad—"

"Shhh. I know, baby. I know. We'll talk as we Travel." She turned to Mrs. Rand. "I'll be right back. Don't worry about this. I will make sure they're okay."

At the thought of Traveling again, an involuntary shudder took over Finn's body. The movement also re-triggered pain. Every joint and muscle seized. "But I can't climb to the tree and she—she has the ring!"

"What—? Never mind. It's fine. It's going to be easy this time. Don't you worry." She grabbed his hand tightly, and the glow of the fireplace turned into the blaring white light that Finn was beginning to recognize all too well.

CHAPTER 28

It was just as Mom promised. The trip was smooth, like he was traveling with young Faith again. Almost like floating. The light was still there, but it was more of a glow now. The roaring sound that Finn had associated with it was just a soft background hum. It droned on in a comforting kind of way, like the sound of tires hitting the seams in the highway while he slept curled up in the backseat of his parents' car.

He could feel Mom reaching out to him. He reached back.

"This must be much easier for you this time, yes?"

"Yeah. It was hard before, but this time when Faith pushed me out—it was horrible."

"She pushed you? How?"

"She just raised her arms and held out her hands . . ." And Finn remembered the terror on Aunt

Billie's face when he had made the same gesture. Aunt Billie must have seen Faith do it to someone.

"Mom, Aunt Billie is working with Doc."

"I know. She doesn't matter right now. Tell me more about being pushed out by Faith."

Finn thought hard, and as he did the slow comforting drone became louder.

"No, never mind. Stop remembering, Finn. We need to stay on track. I was afraid of this. If Faith can push people out of nodes, that complicates things."

Finn began to wonder how much time they had to talk. He felt the need to tell Mom as much as he could. "Mom. I'm so sorry. I let her have the ring."

"What ring?"

"*The* ring. The key! The one you gave to me."

Finn could feel his mother's confusion billowing softly in the warm air around him. Emotions here were tangible. Maybe understanding all of this was just like understanding physics—there was a quantum layer no one could yet comprehend, dark matter yet to be explained.

"Mom?" He desperately wanted her to make things clear.

"Finn. I haven't been there yet. You're going to have to have patience with me. I haven't done any of those things. A lot of what you're saying does make sense, though. I've been working on a plan for some time now."

"Mom . . ." He had to tell her, before he lost the opportunity or the nerve. "She has you. She has a knife."

"A knife?" Her tone was more surprised than frightened. "What would she need that for?"

"She's bad, Mom. She's . . . she's evil."

"No one is all evil, Finn. Remember that. Promise me that you'll remember that."

Finn remembered the look on Faith's face when she had pushed him out of the node. It was hard to imagine that she could be anything but evil. And yet he also couldn't forget young Faith, the way she looked at him when he told her he loved her, the feeling that they'd had a moment of connection that nothing could erase.

"When you get back, you're going to have to trust your father. Will you do that for me?"

"Mom, he's not even there."

"He'll be there. Trust him and follow his lead."

Understanding washed over Finn. Dad had gone somewhere to deal with all this. The library had been a cover story. Wherever Dad really was, he had a good reason for dropping off the radar.

Finn sent her his quiet acceptance through the space between them. He could feel her love and warmth surround him in response. It was an indescribable sensation that his soul would long for for the rest of his life. There was no way to respond to it with words. Even *I love you* would fall short.

"You won't be there when I get back, will you?"

There was no answer, only another wave of love with a deep longing in it this time—so deep that whenever Finn remembered this moment later in his life, his chest would physically ache in response.

CHAPTER 29

Arriving at the node was the same as before. The roar of the light, the blinding, and then the moment of getting used to having a physical boundary again.

He knew without looking that Mom wasn't there. "Gabi?"

It was the first thing he forced his mouth to say. When he opened his eyes he could see her breaking free from someone's grasp to run to him. She crouched down beside him and bolstered him up by wedging her shoulder under his arm. His legs were weak, but with her help he managed to stand.

Mr. Wells was still there. He started to approach them, but a familiar voice said, "No, leave them alone."

It was Doc.

Finn's anger hit him like gale-force wind, overwhelming any fear he had of Wells and his gun. "You did this. You've made her into what she is."

"You have no idea what you're talking about, son."

"Do NOT call me son!" Finn spat out the words like they were poison on his tongue.

He broke away from Gabi and stood on his own, though Gabi still held on to his hand. He was glad of it; he'd rather he be between her and Doc.

"I want you to leave my family alone. You may have fooled Gran, but I know what you are and what you've done."

"Finn, you don't know what I've done or haven't done. It's all different now. Don't you see? You don't know what ISTA has been trying to achieve."

"I. Don't. Care."

"Listen, s—" He corrected himself. "*Finn*, you're going to have to show us how to use the tree. We need it. We need it to stop Faith. We need it to right things in the timeline."

"You stole my sister, you destroyed my family, and now you expect me to *help* you?" Finn pointed at Wells. "I suppose his job is to make me trust you?"

Wells had his gun drawn, his mouth turned down on both sides with determination. Finn had his eyes on Wells's hand when he saw something move farther back in the woods. Something big, coming fast and effortlessly through the smaller tree growth. Doc Lovell was still talking, but Finn wasn't listening. The shadow began to take human form, long legs and arms, a woman striding toward them.

Faith.

She was a bit older than the adult version he'd seen before. Stronger, more full of horrifying purpose. Red hair flying out behind her and a look on her face that was all fury.

Gabi saw her next. Finn only knew because she squeezed his hand tighter. Finn couldn't look away from Faith. She was headed straight for him and he could do nothing to stop her. Running would mean nothing—you can't outrun someone who is ten steps ahead of you. Years ahead of you.

Doc's expression registered defeat before he even turned around. All the muscles in his face seemed to give up at once: terror and resignation born together.

Wells pivoted and held up the small black revolver in defense. Faith kept her eyes trained on Finn as she strode down amidst the dripping green moss. She wore a long green coat made of fabric that seemed like a shiny reflective wool, nothing that Finn had seen before. It billowed behind her, kicking up broken leaves and dried moss in its wake.

She held up one hand toward Wells without so much as blinking. He yelped like a wounded animal. Over before it even began, the scream immediately cut off as every molecule in his body turned to rusty vapor in front of them. He became nothing but a cloud of reddish dust, gently falling down on the forest floor. It was like he he'd been obliterated by a blast from within. Finn saw rings of energy pulsing out from the space where he had been. It looked like magic, but Finn knew better. Understanding came to him as if it had been there all along: Faith had pushed Wells out of this node, molecule by molecule. Pieces of him were strewn through time, never to be put together again.

And now she was coming for Finn.

Gabi screamed, "Run!" She broke free from his grasp and began to tear through the trees.

Finn had no time to stop her, no time to tell her that there wasn't any point. He reached after her to hold her back and missed the hem of her sweater by an inch. He saw Faith hold up her other hand in Gabi's direction and Finn screamed, "NO, DON'T!"

A blast of wind blew by him and he watched as Gabi's body rose into the air, as if an invisible force was gripping her by her neck. Her feet kicked violently and her face turned red.

"Faith, no! I'll give you whatever you want!"

Doc was kneeling on the ground, cowering in front of this adult version of Faith with a mixture of incredulity and fear.

Gabi's body slammed against the nearest tree. She was twenty feet off the ground and pinned by an invisible force, but now she was at least able to breathe. Finn could see her gasping for precious oxygen.

"Please, Faith. You came for *me*," Finn begged.

Faith was in front of him now, looming over him, a foot taller and impossibly powerful. She was decades ahead of him in everything: in knowledge, science, technology, and most of all, Traveling. She could push people out of nodes, and now she was moving atoms around at the flick of a wrist. In all his terror, he couldn't help but feel a small pang of jealousy.

"Tell me how you did it." She spat the words at him. Finn felt them hot against his cheek.

"Did what?"

"Speak! Don't play games! How did *you* Travel?!"

Travel? That was all? He'd used the tree. She knew this. She had been there.

"You just grab hold and hang on. That's . . . that's it," he stammered.

She leaned in close. Her green eyes would have looked so much like Mom's if they had been full of kindness, instead of hate. They were searching his own eyes for something. Whatever she was looking for wasn't there. She was obviously dissatisfied with him. Behind her, Doc yelled out, "Faith, you can't. You can't hurt them."

Gabi's body rose higher against the tree and she let out a strangled yell of pain.

Faith spun on Doc. "You! You are of no significance. You don't even realize it yet, do you? Your plan is dead. Finn took care of that, didn't you, darling brother? *He* took me this time. Thanks to him, I'm now in charge of my own future."

She gave Finn a sly sugary smile. Finn saw the lines on the sides of her mouth. She *was* older than before.

Doc continued, "Faith, please. We never—"

"Do you really think I need to listen to you, dear Uncle William?" She laughed coldly. The sound bounced off the trees. "You tried to use me. You tried to contain *me*!"

The angrier Faith got the more Gabi writhed in pain. Faith didn't even have to look in her direction.

She turned on Finn. "Show me how to use the tree now, or your friend dies."

CHAPTER 30

Finn was desperately trying to come up with ways to buy more time. All he could think about was what happened to Wells.

"Please, Faith. Why would you care about the tree? It's not going to work again. She made it so it only works once." He was making up excuses on the spot, trying to stall her.

Faith pointed with casual cruelty at Gabi, never letting her eyes off Finn. Gabi let out a desperate, strangled cry, and Finn tried to think of the answer that would save her. Words that would satisfy Faith and save Gabi didn't exist.

In his frustration he yelled back. "Why are you asking *me* anyway? I can't Travel. Mom would be the one to know! Mom can teach you how to *make* a portal tree!"

When he saw the look on her face, he realized why Faith had come back for him. She couldn't get to Mom. She must've left, thinking she could come back, and had found herself locked out of the node. Mom had found a way to keep Faith out.

"You can't get to them, can you? You're locked out of the node. That's why you want the tree. Mom pushed *you* out of the node!"

Faith leaned in close to his face, one arm braced against the tree behind him. "She did no such thing! She's not capable. There is no one more powerful than me!" She was screaming at him now, and Finn could tell she was scared.

Then he saw it. Faith's hand, braced against the tree, had begun to shimmer. She was radiating faint waves of energy, the same way Aunt Ev and Aunt Billie had both done when they were doubling in the same node.

Finn shuddered at the thought of two Faiths. If it was true, the second Faith had just arrived. He looked around hesitantly but saw no one.

Faith pushed him away from the tree with tremendous force. He fell hard on a rock and heard a snap, which he was sure was one of his ribs. The pain ripped through his midsection and traveled down his right arm like a lightning bolt.

Faith grabbed hold of the doorknobs and shouted with frustration when that didn't work. She picked Finn up by the back of his shirt and slammed him against the tree. The blow made him lose his breath.

"You do it. You go to her and you learn how to make a portal! NOW!"

Anything. Anything to save Gabi.

She screamed at him, "DO IT!"

He did as he was told, grabbing hold. He waited for the flash and roar of light. Nothing. It wasn't working. He looked up at Gabi, suspended in pain, and wanted to say how sorry he was that he'd brought her here, that it had come to this.

"It doesn't work anymore. I can't make it work!"

Faith stared at him carefully, reading him for any tells of deception. The shimmer on her hand was beginning to move outward, forming a halo around her fingers, moving up her arm. She seemed not to notice.

"You know what I think?" he said. "I think someone out there *is* more powerful than you, and you have no idea who it is."

She growled at him, "You are useless! All of you! None of you are worth my time!"

Faith pivoted toward Gabi. *Or your friend dies.*

Finn blurted out, "You said you can remember all of them. Every single timeline."

She froze, like a deer that smells the hunter. Finn spoke to her back.

"You know killing her won't help you. There's no timeline where killing her makes your life easier. I can promise you that."

Her shoulders stiffened, and Finn felt certain he'd only succeeded in enraging her more. He waited for the pain, waited to become a bloody mist dissipating in the forest.

Instead, Faith walked quickly back toward the tree line, eyeing the woods around her. A small white light began to grow around her head, becoming wider until she disappeared in a blinding, pulsing orb. He wondered if that was what it had looked like when he held on to the tree. He watched, mesmerized, until he heard the sickening thud that was Gabi's body crashing to the ground.

I hate watching it again and again. I hate her. Do you know what it's like for me? No. You don't. You couldn't possibly.

It never gets easier. In fact, the older I get the harder it is to reconcile all I have done. I rendered people into scattered atoms without a second thought. I left a child broken like a doll on the forest floor. And that's just the little you've seen. There is so much more.

Maybe this is my punishment. I'll live these moments of excruciating regret over and over till I die.

I want you to understand, I did change. I swear, I did. In my universe, at least. I don't expect forgiveness. I just want to change what happens next. Not for me. I don't deserve a different fate, but he does.

Finn deserves better.

This time, it has to work.

CHAPTER 31

Gabi was lying there, twisted and broken. Her arm was bent back at a horrible angle, her face down in the dirt. It was every nightmare come to life. Finn rushed to her side, a guttural scream of anguish fighting its way to his lips.

Doc was immediately next to him. "Don't move her, Finn." His voice was shaky. "We don't know how badly she's injured. We need to call for help. They'll need to stabilize her to get her off the mountain."

Finn's first instinct was to jump in front of Doc and protect Gabi from him. Only he had no idea how to save Gabi and Doc did.

Doc leaned in and put two fingers gently on her neck. "Her pulse is steady." He took off his parka and placed it on top of Gabi.

Heart beating, Finn thought. *Not gone. Not yet gone.*

He heard Doc radioing the others in ISTA. He hated relying on this man in any way, but he was relieved that Doc could reach help. ". . . Tell them a child is seriously injured on top of Dorset Peak, needing immediate attention."

Finn kneeled over Gabi, brushed a small leaf free from her hair. One hot tear spilled over the rim of his eye, landed on her brown hair, and glistened there, like a star in the night sky, before disappearing into the strands.

She didn't stir.

He desperately wanted her to wake up and tell him that it wasn't that bad. He wanted her to open her eyes and see him.

"Why isn't she waking up?" he murmured.

Behind him, Doc said gently, "She's had a big blow to the head, Finn."

Finn turned to find Doc watching him, done with the radio. His face was pale and his gray hair was a mess.

"Don't say another word to me. This is all your fault." Finn fought the urge to attack him. Make him pay for all that had gone wrong.

"Finn, the gun wasn't for you. Mr. Wells—he was here for Faith, to protect you from her. Aunt Billie sent us after you two—warned us Faith was coming for you, said you were in danger. We wanted to find you before she could."

Finn again remembered Aunt Billie's fear of him when he'd thrust his palms up toward her in the church. Her memories of raising Faith must be terrible.

"I know what you must think of me, Finn. I'm not a good man. I know what I'm capable of. I've had the distinct opportunity to be told what I have done in alternate timelines. Can you imagine that? Knowing that you're capable of making terrible choices? Having the woman you love most in the world witness some of them and tell you what they were? No. You can't imagine. You're just a kid."

Finn wanted to argue that he wasn't just a kid, but Doc spoke with such despair that it didn't seem worthwhile to split that hair.

"It was you, wasn't it? You dove after her into the quarry that day," Doc said.

"Yes. Are things—different? Better?"

"Better? I only see what I live. And my Beth"—he looked down at his hands—"she's no longer here to tell me what the other possibilities are." He brushed his eye and Finn saw his grief was real.

"You stole Faith from us."

"I thought that I could fix what was going to happen. I thought if we just had a chance to train her—teach her how to use her immense power—if she was given the opportunity to do good, that she would *become* good." He was pacing through the leaves. "Your parents, they knew that in every timeline where they raised her, she rebelled, and terrible things occurred. Beth told me. She and your mother had Traveled forward to see it."

This was new information. Why didn't Mom tell him there were timelines where Faith stayed with them? Timelines where she still turned out broken, evil. He suddenly remembered the photo in Dad's office. The timestamp wasn't from developing the film, it was made by the camera on that day. His father somehow had a relic from another timeline—a timeline where they had Faith longer.

And it still hadn't been enough. "Faith's ability is too much for a child," Doc went on. "She can see even more than Beth and Liz combined. She can see and remember every human choice ever made or not made, the best and the worst of humanity. Liz and Beth knew that nodes were being closed, and while ISTA suspected the Others, your gran first suspected

Faith. Your mother finally admitted to seeing it." He rubbed his eyes, smearing dirt across his sweaty forehead. "Your parents decided not to train her at all. Your mother kept saying they could find a way to contain her."

He stopped pacing and looked directly at Finn. "I had a different plan for Faith. I was going to give her something real to do with her talent. Give her a purpose. She could help us make things right in history. I was so sure it would work."

Finn narrowed his eyes at Doc. "Well, it didn't."

"I know there is so much of the puzzle I'm missing, Finn—but you are, too. Your gran and your mother think the timeline should be left alone. We disagree. We here in Dorset, we've been given a gift! We are *meant* to change things, not just sit by and watch atrocities play out in front of our eyes."

Finn couldn't pretend he didn't see the appeal. All the things he could change for himself, Gran, Mom. Why wouldn't this be a gift they were supposed to use? They were special, chosen.

But he could hear Gabi's voice in his head, cautioning him that it wasn't that simple. One well-intentioned change would set off a chain reaction, with consequences no one could predict. And Mom, what did she tell him? She didn't think they should be the sole arbiters of time.

Doc bent down next to Gabi and checked her vital signs once more.

"Is she okay?"

"The same."

Finn searched his face for reassurance and found none. There was an uncomfortable silence as they both watched Gabi. She still didn't stir.

"What about my dad? Where does he stand on changing the timeline?" Finn asked.

Doc looked up at him and said, "I'm not sure. I don't think he even knows. He agrees with me that we have some sort of responsibility. But he's clouded by his love for you—and Faith."

"Aunt Billie, she's been helping you, even when Gran refused."

He looked genuinely surprised that Finn knew this. "Yes. She's done the Traveling for me. She's a much better Traveler than she ever let on. She even offered to raise Faith as her own, hidden in time." Finn realized that in some other timeline, that had probably ended with Faith raising her hands to Aunt Billie—an imprint that had remained in Aunt Billie's memory. No wonder she'd been afraid of him.

"And Aunt Ev?"

"Solidly against us. She's a hypocrite, though, that one." He threw his hand dismissively into the air. "Says we need to leave the timeline alone, but can't help stealing from her travels. Tells herself it won't make a difference."

He looked up at Finn with glassy, tired eyes. "If you could change this, Finn. If you could make it so Gabi wasn't lying here, you would. Wouldn't you?"

Finn's mind immediately jumped to yes. *YES*, like giant neon letters blinking in front of him. Of course he would. He'd give anything to protect Gabi. He nodded, but even as he did he could see her face earlier this morning. The sun reflecting off her shiny hair. He could hear her worried voice. *"Well, we wouldn't be who we are now, would we? I mean—it's scary to imagine me as someone totally different."*

"Don't you see? We're alike," said Doc. "ISTA has the opportunity to protect our loved ones, along with millions of others. The only thing I've cared about for months is saving Beth. You can't save someone from themselves, though. She wouldn't stop Traveling forward . . ." His voice trailed off, but Finn knew his next thought without him saying it. She wouldn't stop trying to save Finn.

Finn fought the wave of sympathy he felt for Doc. He didn't want to forgive him, but Doc knew what the word *gone* meant, too.

"Anyway, this is bigger than all of us, Finn. You're right: my plan for Faith doesn't seem to have worked any better than the ones your parents tried. She is never all right in any timeline. There are some people, Finn, people who can never be fixed. They need to be *stopped.* That's a task that only men like myself and you are up to. Do you understand what I'm saying?"

Everybody was suddenly calling him a *man* now. He wasn't sure he liked what Doc meant by it.

And yet—if Faith was capable of doing horrible things, why try to save her? Why not try to fight her? Together, as a family, they could win. It sounded like a war was what Faith wanted. Why not give it to her?

Finn looked down at Gabi lying unconscious on the leaves. Yes, it seemed like a natural conclusion. The only logical conclusion for someone who, in every single timeline so far, turned into something twisted and wrong. Had anyone ever seen her turn out good? Mom couldn't even admit to seeing it.

The only solution he could see was to kill her.

Still, forcing herself into his mind's eye was young Faith. The one who held his hand. The one who looked back at him and understood how much he loved her. Doc was talking about 'some people.' That didn't fit at all. Faith wasn't anonymous. She was distinct, specific . . . HIS sister.

He looked at Doc and realized he would never understand. He never Traveled. Doc could only see what Faith was now. Only moments ago Finn was on the mountain with both Faiths—his tiny, trusting and scared baby sister and his broken, angry adult twin. He understood what Traveling did to you now. Faith would always be everything to him all at once. He would not, could not, separate them.

Doc was wrong.

ooo

The search and rescue people came by helicopter. They lowered a man in a small clearing farther up the trail. Finn watched as the man, vibrant in his orange-and-yellow reflective jumpsuit, descended on a cable and then disappeared behind the tree canopy. In seconds he reappeared on the trail, carrying his equipment.

He ran up to them and laid a pack at Gabi's feet. "Are either one of you injured?"

Finn was sure he was. His wrist still hurt and when he breathed in it felt like someone was thrusting a dagger into his ribs. At least one of them must be broken.

He didn't care. All he cared about was Gabi. Anyway, how could he explain that he'd been battered about in a timeless ether, or slammed against a tree by his evil time-traveling sister? He was still trying to find the words to explain it all to himself. He shook his head and saw Doc do the same.

"Tell me what happened." The rescuer looked at Doc, and it became obvious to Finn that neither of them had thought of how they were going to answer that question.

Finn interjected before Doc had a chance to speak. "She climbed the tree to get a better idea of where we were and she fell." Lying did get easier the more you did it. He realized he'd better get used to it. It was going to be a regular part of life now.

"Did you see her fall? How she landed?"

"No," Finn answered.

The man gave Doc a questioning look. Doc shook his head. "No, I didn't see her fall. I'm a doctor. Her airway is intact, contusions on the chest, possible pneumothorax . . ." He paused and glanced at Finn before continuing. "Stable, but GCS is 5 out of 15."

Doc and the rescue worker exchanged a meaningful look.

"I'll stabilize her, and we'll need to bring her about a hundred feet south of here where there's a clearing big enough to cable her up. I'll need your help. Then they'll take her down to Dartmouth, and you can head down to meet the ground team that's on its way to meet you."

"Wait. I can't go with her?" Finn had thought he'd be by her side the whole time.

"No, the helicopter is only equipped to take the injured and the team." The rescuer handed a small device to Doc. "This is a beacon to help the ground team find you."

Minutes later, Gabi was cocooned in what looked like an orange body bag. *No*, Finn thought, *it's like a sleeping bag. That's what it is.*

Finn and Doc helped the rescue worker lower her down the trail. Slowly, carefully, they plodded down the same path he and Gabi had climbed. It felt like days ago now. Finn could hear the helicopter making passes over them. Finally, they came to the small clearing. The rescue worker told them to duck and take shelter as the helicopter came close. Dirt and debris began to kick up from the wind of the blades.

When Finn was able to look again, the man already had a giant cable hook in his hand and was hooking himself and Gabi to it. He was off to the side of her, on a small swing-like pedestal, as they lifted up into the air.

And then Gabi was gone.

CHAPTER 32

The walk down the mountain with Doc was a quiet, torturous march. In some ways it was harder than climbing up. Finn's side hurt with each deep breath and every footfall, and he had to concentrate hard just to stop himself from tumbling forward on the steep trail. He was exhausted and still in panic mode. Gabi falling. Mom left on the mountain. It all felt like it was happening right now. He couldn't convince his body that it wasn't still happening. His heart was pounding and his brain was begging for him to react to a moment that was no longer *now*. Or was it? Was everything now? Maybe that was what Travelers had to live with. Or maybe it was the opposite.

His head began to ache along with his ribs.

He tried not to think anymore. He focused on the pain instead. Dissecting it. Cataloguing it. Taking stock of where it was in his body.

"Finn, are you okay?"

Finn barely grunted in response. Even if he wanted to talk to Doc, which he did not, the pain in his side was too much. He needed to take quick short breaths. Adding conversation was impossible.

They heard them before they saw them. The rescue team called out from below, and the beacon Doc carried suddenly chirped loudly in response, like a loyal digital pet.

"We're up ahead!" Doc yelled.

Finn was relieved until he realized it didn't matter. Even with the rescue team catching up to him, he still had to hike down the rest of this mountain broken and exhausted. He wanted to curl up in the moss and go to sleep. It had been ages since he'd last slept for real. His mind grew fuzzy trying to figure out how many days he'd lived in this one day alone.

The first thing Finn asked was when he'd hear about Gabi. One of the EMTs—a woman with a ruddy, kind face—answered him. "All we know so far is she safely arrived at the hospital and is in the very best care. We have to concentrate on getting you down so you can see her back to good health, okay?"

Looking at Finn skeptically, she offered him water and told him to sit down. Finn was happy to comply. The EMTs covered him with a blanket and asked him what hurt. Finn did his best to communicate. His brain was falling asleep on him. Words weren't coming together the way he wanted them to. One of the rescue workers handed him a bright orange parka and Finn accepted it without protest. As they sat there Finn was sure they were asking him more questions, only he could no longer put the words together to make sense.

"I'm real tired," was all he managed to say.

The rest of the trip down the mountain was a blur. They made him drink water regularly and two people held him up part of the way. His chest felt constricted and he realized that at some point they had bound his middle in bandages. He couldn't remember when.

The darkness was complete now and the mountain grew colder. Finn was glad for the orange parka. It was warm and comfortable and made him want to sleep. The rescuers had helmet flashlights and glowing sticks on their jackets. They passed the hunter's cabin in the dark. Finn wanted them to point a flashlight at the doorway. He wanted to know if the animal skull was still there. He had a sick feeling that it was something Faith had left for him. A warning that he hadn't quite understood till now.

As the trail leveled out he saw the cluster of flashing lights at the bottom of the trailhead. There was a ton of commotion up ahead. Every bone in Finn's body hurt. Even his gums felt bruised from the constant, tooth-rattling impact of his feet against the sloped ground.

The search and rescue team handed him over to an ambulance crew who immediately placed him on a gurney. As he collapsed into it he felt every muscle in his body thank him.

A man was yelling and pushing his way through the crowd toward him. Finn watched groggily as the silhouette resolved itself into someone he knew.

"Dad?"

"I'm here, Finn, I'm here."

As they moved him into the ambulance, Finn's body warred with his mind. He was being poked and prodded, but his body was still willing itself to go to sleep. His mind fought to stay awake. He needed to ask Dad all the questions, if only he could remember what they were.

Dad was by his side and holding Finn's hand tightly in his. "It's okay, son, you did it. You did it."

His father sounded almost victorious. He didn't know! He didn't know that Mom was still lost, that Faith was still evil, and that Gabi was badly hurt. Finn would have to explain how he'd failed.

"Dad, I screwed it up. Everything went wrong."

"You did just fine." He patted Finn's forearm and looked up briefly at the EMT. That was Finn's signal to stop talking. It would have to wait till they were alone. Which was fine with him. He was in no rush to see the look on Dad's face when he had to set him straight with the horrible truth.

He sank into the oblivion of sleep. He dreamed about the peacefulness that was Traveling with Mom, the comforting thrum of the light. He dreamed about the look on young Faith's face when he told her he'd always love her. That moment when he was sure she understood. Her eyes became full of stars, ever-expanding, like the universe. She smiled at him and then became two Faiths, each one staring at the other like a mirror. Then he dreamed of dappled amber sunlight through fall leaves, and then that light went dark. Snuffed out. The dream went from calm to a panicked search for that light.

He woke up in a hospital bed. An uncomfortable device was pressing down on his middle finger. He raised his hand to see what it could be, and his father leapt into view.

"How are you feeling? Don't try to move. Take it easy, you had quite a time up there."

"Where's Gabi?" Finn's voice came out more like a croak. He was thirsty again. Dad reached over for a small plastic pitcher on a side table and poured him some water. Finn refused it with a wave of his hand. "No. Gabi. Tell me."

"She's going to be fine, Finn. Some broken bones, a dislocated shoulder, and a bad concussion. She'll need time, but she's going to be okay."

The pressure of the bandages around his chest melted away for a moment. He could breathe. Gabi was alive. There was that.

"You have a broken rib, some nasty bruising. You were both seriously dehydrated. The doctor says you will be fine and get out of here today, most likely. Gabi will need to be here a bit longer."

Finn didn't want to hear that he would be fine. He didn't deserve to be fine. "Dad, I messed up everything."

"You most certainly did not." He rose up and walked over to the doorway and shut the door gently so as not to make any noise. He came back to the chair beside Finn's bed.

"You showed tremendous courage. I've never been more proud of you, Finn."

"Faith took herself, young Faith—"

"I know. I know all that."

"Dad, you think you know. You don't. Whatever Mom told you I was going to do, I screwed up."

"No, you didn't. Young Faith is still with Mom. I found them. She left a record for me to find. Mom has had some time to make an impact on her. We think it may be enough, Finn. We think she has a chance."

Finn wished he could believe that. But it was hard not to think of all those timelines when Faith had turned on Mom and Dad despite their best efforts. Not to mention the timelines Faith had talked about—the ones where their parents failed her, gave up on her. Still, he tried to imagine a young Faith growing up with all the love Mom could give her. There was a glimmer of hope.

He refocused on Dad. "Where were you?" he asked, but without the resentment that he would've felt a couple of days ago.

"Your mother told me if I stayed nearby I would ruin it all. I would try and shelter you from—from this." He gestured around the both of them at the machines Finn was attached to and the bag of fluids plugged into his arm. "She wasn't wrong."

"She told you what would happen?"

"No. Your mother and I have an understanding. I don't like to know everything about the future, Finn. Not more than I need to. I prefer the past. It's not good to know every outcome—I imagine your sister could tell you that."

Finn was trying to imagine her life, what it could be like inside her head, when he remembered all that his father still did not know.

"Dad! I think Mom may have found a way of shutting Faith out of a node. Faith's angry because she can't get back to Mom and force her to teach her how to use the portal tree."

Dad smiled. "There is no such thing as a portal."

"There is, Dad. Mom left it for Faith. It's a tree on top of the mountain."

"I know that's what Gran told you. But there is no tree."

"Dad, there is! I saw it. I used it! There's this tree—"

"Yes, a tree with two doorknobs on it, only it can't make anyone a Traveler. And a key ring that was a trinket I gave your mother when we were dating. Your mother lied to you. I know that hurts, but don't you see, Finn? You did it. You Traveled! All on your own. You're the first male in the line to be able to time travel. It might have to do with you being the first set of twins or the difficult pregnancy your mom had. You were a rare case, fraternal twins that shared a placenta in the womb. You shared blood . . ."

Ordinarily Finn would've been thrilled to hear his dad talking about science and heredity, but he had it all wrong. "No, Dad. I'm not a Traveler. That's not how it worked. I used the tree and it took me to Mom, and then to the quarry the day Faith disappeared . . ."

"Yes, I remember." Dad was sitting on the edge of the hospital bed now. Still smiling. His clueless optimism was driving Finn crazy.

"That was Mom! She made that happen."

"No, Finn. That was you. Your mother said in nearly every timeline you didn't believe in yourself. She told me we tried to teach you, to tell you the truth from the beginning and guide you through the process. Every timeline where we did that, it resulted in you—well, leaving us. We couldn't bear to lose you. We had to create a scenario where you wouldn't stand in your own way and no one would have any idea that you had the ability."

Finn remembered Traveling with little Faith, how it was easier and he thought it was because she was doing it. Could it really have been him?

As Finn put each puzzle piece together in his mind, the air in the room became heavier, pulsing around him, and threatening to crush him in the middle of the hospital bed.

"You knew? You knew I'd have to go through all of this?" Images of a chessboard rose up in his mind.

"Mom thought up the tree as a device," Dad explained patiently, "to give you courage and, more importantly, to hide your ability from Faith. And also from Gran. Gran was too close to Doc. She had a hard time accepting that he could hurt us. The tree was a ruse. You are the one who locked Faith out of that node, Finn."

It was impossible to make Dad understand. Dad hadn't been there on that mountain. Finn tried to think of the right words to put together in a sentence, to make Dad see that he hadn't done anything at all. The constant beep of the monitor next to his bed wasn't helping his concentration.

"Dad, I don't know how to lock a node! I can't Travel. That wasn't me!"

The beeps became faster and more insistent the more agitated he became.

Dad put his hand to his forehead tenderly. "Calm down. It will all start to make sense. Trust me. You did all the right things."

Finn thought of Adult Faith's rage. "She's going to come kill me. As soon as she figures out—"

Dad gave him the kind of smile you give a small child who doesn't understand. "She doesn't know what you're capable of—only we do. That's the point. She doesn't find out. If she did, you wouldn't be here."

"Dad, I promise you, I did not close Faith out of that node."

"You may have done it inadvertently. Or sometime in the future. You'll figure it all out as you learn more."

The idea of future Finn, Adult Finn, running around in time made his head ache.

"Finn, I know it's going to be hard to get used to, but you do have this ability." Dad held Finn's hand, leaving the little finger clip in place. "And you've been able to keep it a secret. We now have the upper hand. You did it."

The door to the room swung open wide and a cheerful nurse walked in. "How is our patient feeling?"

He's feeling confused, Finn thought. "I'm good. Much better," he said.

"Well, it looks like you'll be going home with your dad in a few hours." She came over and checked the beeping screens.

"Dad, can we go see Gabi?"

"Let's give her a little time to heal. She'll be here a few days more, and her mom is with her now."

Mrs. Rand! Dad said only he and Mom knew, but that wasn't true. Mrs. Rand was there when he landed in her living room. Why didn't Dad know about Mrs. Rand?

He remembered Mom's words: *You have to keep secrets from those you love the most, and sometimes you have to lie.* Finn began to wonder how much Mom had told *Dad*.

The nurse gave Dad some information about the discharge process and left.

Finn whispered, "Dad, you already know, don't you? You know that Mom isn't coming back?"

"Yes." He looked down at his hands. Finn didn't have to see his eyes to know that they were full of pain. "She lied to me as well. She didn't tell me that part of the plan. I wouldn't have agreed to it and she knew it. I've been researching her whereabouts for the last few weeks, checking death records and old graveyards."

"Did you find her . . . grave?" Finn swallowed hard.

"No. I did not."

"But she's never coming back, is she?" Finn asked.

"Once you spend time around Travelers, you begin to realize there is no such thing as never."

CHAPTER 33

The ribs still hurt, and it would take a while before Finn felt like his old self. Overall, a few days of sleep and rest had helped. He stared up at his bedroom ceiling and tried to believe in a world where he could make a huge difference. Everything he had experienced in the last few days was scientifically implausible, but he knew it was real. If he could believe in time travel, making the leap to believing in himself shouldn't be all that hard.

Still, it was. Infinitely hard.

He heard the doorbell chime and Dad's quick footsteps as he left his paper-strewn office to answer it. Soft muffled voices followed and then a knock on his bedroom door.

"You have a visitor, Finn."

For a split second he hoped it was Gabi, but it

was far too soon. She wouldn't be up and about for at least another week.

"I came in by way of the front door this time." It was Aunt Ev, smiling ear to ear. She was less bundled up than when he'd seen her last, and there was no shimmer around her. This put Finn at ease. One Aunt Ev was more than enough.

She pulled his desk chair out and took a seat. "I'm not here to ask any questions." She nodded at Dad, who was leaning against the doorjamb with his arms crossed and a matching grin on his face. "I don't even want to know. I've always preferred conjecture. I'm just here to say, if you ever need me, for anything"—she opened her eyes wide for emphasis—"I'll be there. No questions asked. Understand?"

"Yes, I do." Finn smiled.

Dad excused himself with an offer to whip up lunch. Aunt Ev thanked him and watched him go.

"Good. Now that we're alone, let me tell you some stories I've been dying to tell all these years."

She went on for at least an hour. Finn had to stop her several times because he was laughing so hard, it made his ribs hurt even more. It was so good to laugh, though—he almost didn't mind the pain. She told him about her Travels within her own lifespan and even further back. Unlike Gran and Mom, she couldn't move forward in time, so she made the most of her trips backward. She fired up his tablet and showed him how she'd been caught on film in a Charlie Chaplin movie talking into a cell phone. "That was stupid of me. I accidentally wandered into the shot. I wasn't actually speaking to anyone of course, just recording some personal notes." He looked at the grainy video carefully, and sure enough, there was Aunt Ev pausing in the background and speaking into what looked like an early model mobile phone. "Easy enough to explain away as an archaic hearing device and a mumbling old lady, but geez, was your gran mad at me!"

He knew what she was doing. She was showing him the lighter side of what they were. That it wasn't all the horrors of reliving your family's worst days over and over again.

"Aren't you afraid you'll change things?" he asked. "Isn't that what you're supposed to be avoiding?"

"I've been around long enough to know that there's a persistence to it, Finn. I'm not sure why, but it's awfully hard to shift the overall arc of time. You make a change and things have a way of working out pretty much the same. Not always, mind you, but I'd say nine out of ten."

Finn did not like those odds. He had to agree with what Doc said: Aunt Ev seemed a little reckless. Still, she certainly made it sound fun.

"How do you even *know* it's turned out the same?"

"Excellent question! Changing the past, it's supposed to be the perfect crime, isn't it? There are no witnesses. Once the past is changed, everyone accepts that as true history, right?"

That sounded logical. Finn nodded.

"Except your mother could see where things were altered from the *prime* imprint. She never would've let me get away with doing any lasting damage. She didn't hesitate to sound the alarm when someone was changing the timeline—namely, Doc, Billie, and the Others. Most of ISTA didn't believe her. That's when your parents retreated into themselves. They became quiet and secretive, didn't trust anyone."

"How much did they trust *you* with?"

"Not much at all. But I like it that way. It makes for a much more comfortable existence."

"So what's your opinion on—Faith?"

"All I can say is, it'd be a shame for her talent to be put to the wrong use. The daughter . . ." She paused here and corrected herself with a knowing grin. "The *child* usually has what talents the mother had, and then some. My mother couldn't travel backward beyond her own time of birth. I can. And your gran was the first one to go forward in time, only it was very sparingly. It cost her dearly, health-wise."

They both sat quietly for a moment, missing Gran.

Then Ev looked around the room, clearly searching for a distraction, and fixed her gaze on the periodic table of elements on the wall behind him. "You know, I think they're missing marble."

"Marble isn't an element."

"Well, I can't claim to know science the way you do. All I'm saying is maybe they should be studying it more closely."

Finn didn't want to sound disrespectful, but he knew that marble was made up of ordinary elements like calcium and carbon. Aunt Ev must have read his mind, because she gave him a sly grin.

"Did it help you at all? The grounding stone?"

"I don't know, maybe . . ." He thought about the pain of being thrown off the node completely. How he thought about the stone . . . but no. It was Gabi. He said her name over and over and somehow there was this great big ball of light . . . Gabi's dream!

It was Gabi's dream in third grade that brought him home!

"Well, I still say there's no Traveling without Dorset marble. Where do you think it all went to back in the day, all that stone from the quarry?"

Finn tried to focus. "Well, they sold it."

"Yep, up and down the east coast. Buildings that still stand till this day."

Now that he thought about it, Faith had mentioned it too—how in one timeline, she'd been far away from home but had used Dorset marble to Travel. "The Others! That would explain why they can Travel even though they're not in Dorset."

"That's my, what do you call it . . . hypothesis? That's it."

So many new ideas floating around in his head—he could only half-grasp them at best. "It can't be magic stone, Aunt Ev."

"Magic, science. Call it what you wish. You agree that there is still a lot that humans don't know about the natural world?"

"Sure . . . I think you may be on to something—"

"Of course I am! Science may not be able to prove that magic exists, but I'm going to guess that it can't prove it doesn't."

"You know, that's the kind of stuff Gabi says all the time."

She grinned. "Well now, I'm beginning to like that squawky little bird more and more."

ooo

The next few days went by in a comforting blur of playing video games, reading, and sleeping. Finn's thirteenth birthday was a quiet one, but he didn't mind. He was used to it. Dad got him a cake and Aunt Ev stopped by to help celebrate. She gave Finn some new books on physics and his own vintage watch. Finn raised an eyebrow at her and she immediately put both hands up in surrender. "Got it online. I swear!"

The best part of the day was chatting with Gabi online. She wasn't able to visit yet, but she was doing much better. Finn kept the conversation light—they talked about books she was reading, and she poked fun at him for being a teenager. He was going back to school before her and promised to fill her in on what happened each day. It was as if they'd both agreed to discuss more important matters in person.

Finn tried several times to Travel. He concentrated and hoped to see the threads of time, the glowing nodes. Each attempt was more disappointing than the last. He had somehow expected everything to fall into place after his birthday, but it didn't. He kept this piece of information to himself.

Dad barely left the house and continued his work researching Dorset residents in the late 1800s, looking for any other signs of Mom and Faith. He had already found a mention of a widow with a small child who was teaching at the one-room schoolhouse. Their name was one that he and Mom had agreed upon as a code if the worst were ever to happen. That was the only clue so far, though, and Dad was tirelessly searching for more.

Dad didn't tell Finn specifically what he was trying to find, but Finn saw the pages and pages of old Dorset death records. If Mom stayed and never came back, there would be a record of her death.

Finn comforted himself with logic. She could still find a way out and come visit them, even if she had to return to the past. She could show up here any minute.

She couldn't ever be truly gone. Could she?

He peeked in on Dad and asked how it was going. The office was still in shambles. Dad saw the look on Finn's face and assured him he knew what was in each and every teetering pile.

"Over there is information on the cheese factories. They were big in the late 1800s. In that pile is correspondence of summering residents. Dorset had already become a summer boarding resort. Your mother picked a fine time to take up residence. Business booming! She'll be okay."

Something about his tone told Finn he was trying to reassure himself more than Finn.

Finn looked up at the shelf behind him for the photo. "Where's the other picture you had?"

"What picture?"

"Um, never mind." He wouldn't press now. Maybe in this altered timeline it caused Dad too much pain to have it there. Finn's head was beginning to throb.

"You feeling okay? Can I get you something?"

Finn couldn't help but notice that Dad was making a huge effort. It took a lot to make Dad come out from behind the books, and now Finn understood why. It wasn't history to him. It never was. Once you lived with a Traveler, everything was now.

The concerned look on Dad's face reminded him of the day at the quarry. How Dad had called him a man.

Finn had been so wrong about Dad. His father

loved him, loved him with his whole heart. Finn wanted to apologize for the way he'd acted, but he knew it would come out as a choked sob. He wasn't ready to cry yet. He didn't want to make Dad cry either. The air in the room became even more oppressive.

"I just need some air. I'll be fine." He made for the door, pretending to feel much better than he actually did.

"Okay then, I'll stop and make us some dinner in a bit," Dad called after him.

"Yep." Finn held on to the walls for support and made his way to the back door. He needed air, that was it.

CHAPTER 34

Out on the patio, Finn took a deep breath, and as the cold oxygen filled his lungs he felt better. He sat in the nearest lounge chair and pulled his sweatshirt sleeves over his hands for warmth. The air smelled of firewood and dead leaves.

He could see the space in the tree line where Aunt Ev had led him and Gabi. It was a lifetime ago. For a moment, the memory of Faith striding through the trees and brush on the mountain surfaced in his mind. It sent chills through his body. No matter what Dad or Aunt Ev said, his mind played the fears in a loop. She could come after him anytime.

He pushed the thought out of his head. He wasn't going to let Faith make him afraid of his woods.

Anyway, if Dad was right, he had other things to worry about. Dad and Aunt Ev were so sure he was going to develop some impressive Traveler powers. What if they were wrong? Nothing was happening for him. He touched the smooth stone Aunt Ev had given him, snug in his pocket.

He hoped he wouldn't suddenly wake up in another time by accident. Aunt Ev had told him that it was only the last three generations that were able to control it at all. Some of his ancestors didn't even realize they were Travelers. They thought they were having terrible dreams or being haunted by ghosts. It made sense; if you suddenly woke up in a tavern one hundred years earlier and saw all these people milling about, a non-scientific mind could imagine they were ghostly visions. Okay, so maybe even a *scientific* mind would be fooled. Still, he planned to take notes of anything strange and keep his wits about him. Assuming anything would even happen at all.

The truth was he couldn't shake the feeling that someone else was responsible for the few battles he had won.

He laid his head back and looked at the gray sky. It would be dark soon. He closed his eyes and thought about Gran. How much easier all this would be if she were here to guide him.

"Hello, Finn."

He didn't even have to open his eyes—he knew it was her. But his eyes wanted to see. She was there in front of him on the patio. As real and alive as if she had never gone.

"Gran!"

"I told you I'd see you again."

He swallowed a lump in his throat. "Why . . . why didn't you tell me sooner?"

She smiled weakly. "I honestly thought I had more time. How's that for irony?"

She cautiously laid herself in the lounge chair next to his, sighing deeply.

"Are you okay?"

"No. I'm dying, but you knew that already."

Finn sat up quickly in a panic. "Gran—"

"Now you wait. Don't speak. Tell me. You did it, didn't you? You got Faith away from the quarry?"

"Yes, but—"

The skin around her eyes crinkled up as she smiled wide. She could smile two ways. He knew when she did it with her eyes, that she was truly happy.

"Your mother, what a sharp one. I raised her right and she did good by you, too."

"There's more, Gran."

She put up one slender hand to stop him.

"Listen, you're going to need to know some important things about talking to Travelers. You don't say more than you need to. You don't say much at all. You listen. You wait for the questions. You think about when the Traveler is from before you speak. You understand?"

"I think so." She was cautioning him not to tell her too much, but what did it matter now? "Where—I mean, when are you?"

"For me, it's the night I go. Late in the evening after you've gone to bed. I've arranged for a younger me to talk to you in the morning."

"Yes, we've met."

"It must seem strange to you, the way I talk to my past and future selves—we have a lot of loose ends to tie up, and we often recruit ourselves to help. In fact, I was talking to yet another Me when I sent you off to Gabi's house that morning."

Finn remembered the hushed murmurs through the door.

She took a deep, rattling breath and coughed. "I attempted far too many tricks tonight. You got me thinking, with that many-interacting-worlds theory. I thought maybe we keep failing because there is more than one Faith, that maybe she's found a way to hop universes, like you said. If I could only check—well, I found it. It's out there and it's possible to make the jump."

"You found a next-door universe?"

"All this time, we were operating on the basis of multiple timelines. We were short-sighted. There are multiple universes, *each* with multiple timelines. I only got a glimpse of what's next door." She sighed sadly. "I also got a glimpse of what Billie and Will were up to in ours."

"And then you left me the note."

"Yes."

Finn turned his head away from her, preferring to ask this question to the forest in front of him. "So then, this is the last time for us, isn't it?"

"Yes. This is the last time."

Finn reached over the space between their two lawn chairs and grabbed her hand. He held on tight. Gran squeezed back and swallowed hard before continuing.

"Now," she had that lecturing voice, "remember when we spoke about the butterfly theory the other night?"

"Yes, Gran. It's part of chaos theory." He couldn't help thinking she was still in "the other night."

"Right. In time travel, it's the big, fat, scary warning. It's the belief that one small change can create a disaster of epic proportions. Well, it's hogwash. The most important thing you need to know is that time is persistent. She's stubborn. Time is one stubborn—" She took a deep breath and pursed her lips like she was angry with some invisible creature standing before them on the patio. "Well, let's just say she cannot be persuaded, shall we? It's not about the beat of a wing or catching a later bus. You think you've shifted something, and then something else happens to bring about the original outcome."

He remembered Aunt Ev saying the same thing.

"Then why even care? Why try and change anything?"

"Here's the key, here's the only thing Time listens to, Finn. What matters is how people affect people."

Finn's mind flashed back to his swelling stars. It was like the universe kept trying to tell him something in a language he didn't understand.

"I know the way you think," Gran said gently. "You think you have a staggering mathematical problem in front of you. You're thinking about all the permutations you'll have to figure out. None of this can be solved with equations or software.

What I'm trying to tell you is, it's not the data, it's the people. It's the choices they make—choices to be kind, choices to see and not look away. Those are the real factors. That's what tilts the equation. It has never been the beat of a butterfly wing, it's the beat of a human heart. If you want to change time, you must change hearts. Remember that, Finn."

She squeezed his hand again, weaker this time but with the same tenderness. Finn blinked hard, staring at her wristwatch.

"People will tell you Faith needs to be stopped at all costs. That she's a twisted, evil thing that needs to be erased."

"Have you *met* her lately, Gran?"

"Oh, I've had many a glimpse. I know what she is and what she's capable of. I have no doubt. I only ask you to remember what she once was—and know that you've already changed her. You've planted a seed in her that she can't ignore."

Finn thought about Faith's small trusting face, still smeared with tears and dirt, her piercing green eyes staring at him, connecting them.

"How can you possibly know that?" he asked.

"Because this time, when I've come here to check on you, *you are alive*."

Hearing that Faith had killed him in other timelines shouldn't be a surprise. It didn't even bother him so much. He knew the dangers that lay in wait for him now, and somehow he no longer felt afraid. What bothered him was that his loved ones had to keep witnessing it. His heart ached the most for Mom. The chess game she had been forced to play was no game at all.

It wasn't fun for him either.

"There was no magic portal, Gran." He wanted her to know. She had been so proud of Mom for making it. Deep down, in that selfish place that resides in all of us, he wanted some company in his disillusionment. "It's just a tree."

"Oh, I'm not so sure about that. Your mother created it. We both believed in it and it worked. Sounds magical to me."

He was sure that was not solid evidence and was about to say so until he realized there was no point in looking for proof of magic.

"I know you're still worried about what's next. Will is not going to be a problem. He'll be leaving Dorset, and Aunt Billie left for New York today."

That didn't comfort him much, especially when he considered what Aunt Billie might know. It was more than just the way she hid her Traveler powers; it was the way she had been afraid of him in the church. For that brief second, she'd suspected he could Travel, too.

"Aunt Ev and your father will run ISTA now, and maybe in time"—Gran gave him a hopeful smile—"you'll take over?"

"If that's what you want, Gran."

She sighed and let go of his hand. "It's my time, Finn. I want you to know I'm so proud of you."

Finn jumped up out of the chair. He wanted to stop her, hold her back from going anywhere.

She did not rise. She lay there calmly and smiled. She began to glow, but not with the white light that Finn knew so well from his few travels. The light was bluish and calm. It started at Gran's heart and was growing outward in all directions.

"Gran, I don't want to do this without you. I—I love you."

He could no longer hear the words coming out of her mouth, but he could read her lips. She mouthed the same three words back to him and then, just like that, Finn was standing there alone, looking at an empty lounge chair.

CHAPTER 35

It was another week before Gabi was able to be outside on her own. Her arm and shoulder were held in place with a sling. She had to walk slowly, but they could finally enjoy a visit to the Union Store and maybe get the last of the morning bagels.

"You should fear and respect me now. I'm part machine." She pointed to the place in her arm where the metal pins had to be inserted and waggled her eyebrows at him. Finn gave a weak smile. He couldn't laugh at Gabi's injuries.

"I know what you're thinking and you're wrong," she said.

"Oh? Why don't you tell me what I'm thinking?" He wasn't as perturbed as he sounded—this was part of their regular game. Life was returning to some semblance of normal.

"You're thinking this is somehow your fault, and it's not. It's Faith's fault. No one else's. Besides, I knew what I was getting into." She jutted her small, sharp chin forward defiantly.

None of that made him feel any better. It only meant he had to be more careful. "Your mom knew about me, Gabi. All along."

"She told me."

Finn was stunned. "When?"

"Not until I woke up in the hospital. She told me how you appeared in my living room back in the third grade. It freaked her out. Don't worry, she realizes how important it is to keep the secret."

"Do you know why I was there? It was the night of your dream. The ball of light dream."

"What? How could you possibly know that?"

"You brought me home, Gabi. Your ball of light, your third-grade dream. That's how I found my way back."

He had never seen Gabi at a loss for words before. It was fun to witness.

"Huh," was all she said, but he could see her mind was hard at work, trying to solve an equation of her own.

They were quiet for a few moments more until

Finn changed the subject. "So I guess your mom has been secretly helping my mom for a long time."

"Yeah, she made all her Traveling clothes, for when she'd go to different times. Mom wasn't just working for the theater."

"I figured that. They acted like good friends. But how? She's not even part of ISTA."

Gabi stepped closer to him. "We should probably take the volume down a notch."

Finn looked around. The green was fairly empty this morning except for a few straggling leaf peepers. He waited till an old woman limping toward the post office was well out of earshot before he spoke again.

"I'm just saying, our moms barely ever hung out together."

"Mom said that was part of the arrangement. She didn't want anyone to know about their friendship. It gave her a secret ally outside of ISTA. They actually met in New York, and your mom got my mom the job at the theater. She's why we moved here in the first place."

Finn's mouth hung open in surprise.

"I know. Sneaky, huh?" She said it with pride though. She clearly had a newfound respect for her mom.

They walked past the historic society and the post office. The marble sidewalks were not as impressive in the daytime, and here the slabs were uneven due to the shifting of the soil. Tourists would often trip. Locals knew where the hazards were by heart.

"You know, Gabi, you were right."

"Of course I was. About what?"

"You were the difference this time. I think the reason I'm even here is because you were with me. You found the tree, you brought me home. I owe you."

"Phsh." She nudged the grass seam between the marble slabs with the toe of her sneaker.

"Anyway, I want you to know, you can back out any time you want. This isn't going to get easier."

"No. Absolutely not!" She raised her good arm and made a fist. "We're going to beat her together, Finn!"

Finn took a deep breath. "What if I told you we're not supposed to beat her? That we have to win her back?"

"Ha! Like that's possible!" She kept walking and Finn held back. Realizing he was no longer by her side, Gabi turned. "You're not serious?"

"I have to try. I can't give up on her, Gabi."

"Finn, she's horrible! You saw what she did! Mr. Wells and then . . ." She winced at the memory. It had to have been painful, so much so that she couldn't finish her sentence.

Finn jumped in where she stopped. "I know. I'm furious at her for everything she's done. Especially to you. But there are reasons she's turned out this way. If Traveling is this hard for me, I can't imagine what it's been like for her."

Gabi clearly wasn't convinced. Finn needed her on his side. It would take time, that's all.

"Gabi, there's one more thing. Something I haven't told anyone."

"You promised you'd tell me everything!" Finn was sure if her arm wasn't in a sling she'd have both hands on her hips.

"And I am! Listen, I can tell when someone is doubling in their own timeline."

"You mean the stutter-step thing?"

"No, only the Traveling version does that, and only if they're too close to their initial. Aunt Ev and Aunt Billie, when they were each doubling, or visiting their own timeline, their *initial* would get all shimmery. They would get surrounded by waves of energy. It looks like the waves of heat that come off a street on a summer day. While we were up there, by the tree, Faith started to shimmer the exact same way."

"I didn't see that."

"Well, I think I'm the only one who can see it. Aunt Ev didn't mention it and neither did Gran."

"What can that mean, that Faith shimmered?"

"Well, I think it means that another version of Faith was there. Watching. I think she's working against herself. I think she's the one who closed the node for Mom. Everyone thinks it's me, but I didn't close the node, Gabi. I haven't been able to do *anything*." He looked around cautiously, noting how many people were close enough to overhear: a family with a toddler, the thin elderly woman in front of the bank. He lowered his voice to a whisper. "Somewhere or some*when*, there's a version of Faith who's trying to do the right thing."

Gabi looked skeptical. "Maybe. I mean, I hope that's true. But you *can* Travel, Finn. You can see people shimmering where others can't, and you're still doubting yourself? What more proof do you need?"

"I don't know, how about actually Traveling when I want to? I've been trying and nothing's happened."

"We should go back to the mountain. It might work for you up there."

"Maybe. I don't know if that'll be enough. I don't know if *I'm* enough."

"No one ever knows that! Apparently not even time travelers." She gave him a sympathetic smile. "C'mon, I'm starving and all this walking is making me tired."

He'd forgotten this was her first outing. Even though it was a short walk to the green from her house, she was probably pushing herself.

They headed toward Union at a slower pace. Finn's mind was still a bunch of cogs turning in opposite directions. It was like he was missing something in the equation, something obvious. Maybe it wasn't all about genetics and equations—what if it was a combination of factors? He began to think of all the things that had moved him the last few weeks. Every time, he felt a shiver or deep connection to something bigger than himself. He pictured Gabi in the field of ferns, the changing carpet of leaves under his feet, the marble, the stars in the night sky and the ones in his dream. Aunt Ev's voice echoing in his head: "*Much further back.*"

Suddenly, everything shifted. He found himself

unsteady and reached out to Gabi for balance. It was as if the ground were sinking slightly with every step. He started to feel a bit queasy.

Gabi's eyes were wide with shock. She was staring at the ground below them. "Uhhh, Finn?"

The white stone had begun to bend and morph under his weight like putty. His shoes had created indentations in the rock that should have taken years of wear to form. He took two more experimental steps and looked back. The soft depressions sprang back up, as if the footprints were made in foam, not stone. He stopped, bent down, and studied the marble, tracing the pads of his fingers across the cold, smooth surface.

As his fingers trailed across the stone he had the feeling that the world was suddenly rendered into focus.

It was sharp. Clear. It was like someone had finally turned the lenses the right way. His edges were no longer blurry.

He looked up at Gabi. Her mouth finally found the words, "How did you . . .?"

He had no answer for her. It was nothing he could put into words. It wasn't magic, it wasn't science. It was . . . everything. Elements, electricity, love, air, hope, atoms—he was aware of it all. That was the key: you had to accept it all.

He realized something else too, the all-too-familiar feeling that he was being watched. He stood up and scanned the scene around him. The leaves picked up and whirlygigged around his feet, swirling up around him to his shoulders like an embrace, then floated away. He watched them whirl down the sidewalk, toward the bank. Toward the old woman he had seen earlier.

They locked eyes. He knew those eyes as well as his own. She said nothing, but her words echoed inside his head just the same.

Happy birthday, Finn. I left you a present.

She gave him a smile that Finn instantly recognized. He had seen it with Gran, with Mom, and in flashes of childhood memories. *I moved it, by the way. It's in your closet. I thought it would be too hard on Dad.*

He knew what the present was. He had already found it, held the picture in his hands.

It was like she read his mind and showed him the timestamp in his memory. *In some of our timelines we spend more time together. I wanted you to know.*

New vague memories filtered into his brain. A Faith, five or six, playing with him at the quarry.

Both of them much older, laughing in the backseat of Dad's old car. A happier Faith was shown to him before a flash of the one he met on the mountain.

Steer clear of her, will you? It's a long time till she becomes me.

She turned toward the alley between the bank and the post office, though Finn still heard her thoughts.

I have to go back to my own world. It's up to you now. You are the first boy Traveler—but more importantly, you are Finn. And that on its own is enough. I couldn't have asked for a better brother.

She disappeared into the alley. Finn instinctively took one step forward, but stopped when he saw a calm bluish light glow briefly from between the two buildings.

He turned back to Gabi. She was still on her knees examining the fading marble footprints with her good hand. She hadn't seen Faith at all.

"So are you going to explain to me the science behind *this*?"

"I . . ." he looked back at the alleyway and then back to Gabi. "No, it doesn't need explaining. It just . . . is."

Gabi beamed at him.

He grabbed her good arm and led her up the Union's wooden stairs as casually as if it was any other day.

He could swear the light of the world was glowing amber. It was as if he could almost see it, hear it. Universes were expanding, stars were being born, and people's hearts were changing in each and every world.

Faith didn't know. She had no idea for the longest time, and when it finally dawned on her, it was too late. You may be wondering, how can there be such a thing as "too late" for someone who has the command of both the past and the future?

It's very simple. You can't stop what grows inside of you. Regret and shame settle and fester. What grew inside me, more powerful than either of those, was love. I finally recognized that's what I was getting from Finn all these years. He never stopped trying to save me, in every timeline, in every universe.

So here I stand, watching that horrible young woman I once was stomp around the wood in a rage. She is still in disbelief that someone has bested her.

"It's impossible! No one is more powerful than me!" she hisses as she kicks up dirt and leaves in her wake. And the amusing thing is, she's right. The only one who could truly fool her was me—herself. Finn wouldn't have been able to do this part all on his own. Not yet at least.

You want an ending, don't you? You want to know what happens to Finn and Gabi. Silly, you're assuming I know! The thing is, we never truly know, do we? As Gran said, time is stubborn, but the hearts change. Oh, if I could only show you. They swell, they burst, they grow, and like stars, they sometimes burn with a brilliant white heat and die. Sometimes they even change in one universe and not another. I could tell you what is probable, but there's no fun in that. Why discuss math and probability when you can watch an entire lifetime unfold instead?

That wretched fool has no idea what her brother is capable of. I've kept her busy looking in all the wrong directions, and maybe, just maybe, I have bought myself a small sliver of redemption?

No. I mustn't hope for that. All that matters is that Finn's secret is safe. She never finds out what he can do. Well, not until she becomes me.

And oh, my dear girl, I know what lies ahead for you. That transformation is going to hurt. Regret is a harsh tutor. But how utterly eye-opening it is to discover that all through time, in every permutation of every universe, in defiance of all probability, you were unconditionally loved by one person.

That kind of knowledge changes you.

AUTHOR'S NOTE

And you, dear reader, I bet you want to know how much of this you can believe. Well, I'll tell you this much. Dorset is a real place, with real people. The tree with two doorknobs exists at the top of a scarred marble mountain. You can find it at the crossroads of two trails near the summit. Only a handful of people know it's there.

And now you know.

If you look hard enough you'll also find Aunt Ev popping up where she shouldn't. You can find all sorts of things, no matter where your particular universe happens to lie. You must work for your knowledge, though. It takes time to see the whole picture.

And while you may never have as much time as Faith did, there is always enough time to look again.

ACKNOWLEDGMENTS

I am lucky enough to reside in a universe full of brilliant and kind fellow Travelers. This book would not exist without my agent Linda Epstein, who believed in my work from day one. To my editor, Amy Fitzgerald, who skillfully navigated every timeline with me, and to everyone at Carolrhoda and Emerald City Literary who decided to take this journey with me, thank you.

Thank you to the wonderful people of Dorset, Vermont, who welcomed this flatlander with open arms. The Barrows House and The Dorset Inn, where many of these words were written. A special thank you to the lovely people at Dorset Union Store and Jon Mathewson of the Dorset Historical Society, who provided me with space to research and answered all my tedious historical questions with unending enthusiasm. Vermont Department of Public Safety Search and Rescue Coordinator Neil VanDyke and Trauma Surgeon Dr. Kris R. Kaulback for helping me get Gabi off the mountain. Special thanks to Dr. Colin Bischoff for answering the finer points of physics and time travel.

Thanks to my Highlights family: Jennifer Jacobson, Amanda Jenkins, Nancy Werlin, Melissa Wyatt, and finally, the sparkling Sarah Aronson, for being the best mentors (yes, I said mentors) and friends I could ask for. Thank you to George and Kent Brown, Jo Lloyd, Alison Green Myers, and everyone at the Highlights Foundation for giving this weary Traveler a second home. To all my workshoppers who trusted me with your worlds, thank you.

My Vermont College of Fine Arts mentors who traveled to untamed universes with me, Rita Williams-Garcia, Coe Booth, Susan Fletcher and Leda Schubert, I hope I have made you proud. And to Franny Billingsley, who was right about so many things, thank you.

To my Secret Gardeners and VCFA family, especially Kekla Magoon, Jess Rinker, Miriam McNamara, Laura Sibson, Cordelia Jensen, Laurie Morrison, Katie Mather, and Melanie Fishbane, thank you.

To my friends and first readers who cared for Finn from the beginning: MaryWinn Heider, AmyRose Capetta, Mike Waxman, Christine Danek, Joanne Fritz, Laura Parnum, Amy Beth Sisson, Nicole Wolverton, Hilda Burgos, Martha Bullen, The Book Babes of the Main Line and the indomitable Jenny Gill, who literally climbed the mountain with me, my unending gratitude.

I am forever indebted to my fellow Highlights workshop teacher, VCFA classmate, beta-reader and friend, Rob Costello. Your friendship, deep insight, unending empathy, and brilliant advice are invaluable to me. You are a true Traveler.

Thank you to my mother, Margaret Valentine, my grandmother, aunts, mother-in-law, and all the strong women I call family, for passing on formidable mitochondrial DNA. I get my power from you. A special thank you to my aunt, Elizabeth Steinach, who made it possible for me to write and study by covering for me at home.

And last, because they are first in my heart, to my daughter Lexie, who always has faith in me. And my first reader and partner in all the universes, David. You are my grounding stones.

QUESTIONS FOR DISCUSSION

1. In what ways has Faith's death affected Finn over the years? Find two or three examples.
2. Why does Finn doubt that the women in his family can time travel? What changes his mind?
3. Compare and contrast the three Sykes sisters: Gran, Ev, and Billie. How have they each chosen to use their unusual gift?
4. In what ways are Gabi and Finn different? In what ways are they similar?
5. Gabi says that even if she could change the timeline to prevent her brother from dying, she wouldn't do it, because so many other things would change. If you could time travel, would you try to change something in your life or in history? Why or why not?

6. Finn's mom tells him that no one is wholly evil. Do you agree? Why or why not?
7. Faith can see every timeline and every possible way a situation can play out. Some of those possibilities made her very angry with her parents. What do you think they were?
8. What is Finn's relationship with his dad like at the beginning of the novel? What does Finn learn about his dad that changes the way he sees him?
9. Finn is uncomfortable with Doc calling him a man. Why do you think Doc is so insistent that men should control what happens with the timeline?
10. Why does Finn ultimately decide to not give up on Faith?
11. For most of his life, Finn has believed he is a disappointment to his parents, a poor substitute for Faith. Even when he learns he can Travel, he still feels insecure. What do Gran, Gabi, and Old Faith have to say about this?
12. In every timeline and every alternate universe, Finn continues to love and believe in Faith. What effect does this ultimately have on Faith?

ABOUT THE AUTHOR

Nicole Valentine writes young adult books about the crossroads of science and magic in our world. Outside of fictional world-building, you can find her walking around with a hawk on her arm or wrangling two giant dogs named Merlin and Arthur. She resides outside of Philadelphia with her family.